Roy Chaney's first novel, *The Ragged End of Nowhere*, won
the Tony Hillerman Prize for best debut mystery set in the
American Southwest. He lives in Kansas City, Missouri.

SEVEN TIMES DEAD

ROY CHANEY

280
STEPS

A 280 Steps Paperback

Copyright © 2016 by Roy Chaney

ISBN 9788283550122

www.280steps.com

1

They came for me at dawn.

The scrape of the key in the lock startled me. I rolled off the cot as the cell door swung open. Two French police officers in blue fatigues and billed caps stood aside while I stepped into the hallway.

One of the officers was a broad-shouldered man with dark beard stubble. The other was a young woman with chestnut-colored hair tied up under her cap. The policewoman's pistol hung in a black leather shoulder holster, while the stubbled man carried his automatic in a holster that was strapped to the center of his chest.

I told them that I wanted to see Brissac, the police inspector who had first questioned me.

The policewoman said, "We're going for a ride."

They escorted me out into the courtyard behind the station. A Peugeot squad car identical to the one that had brought me to the police station was parked at the back door. The engine was idling and a third police officer sat behind the wheel. The stubbled policeman motioned for me to get into the back seat. He climbed in after me, while the female officer got into the passenger seat in front.

The car doors slammed shut.

No one spoke.

We had to wind through the center of Nice to get to the highway. After ten minutes in traffic the driver cut down a narrow side street lined with dingy shops and dark apartment buildings. Without warning a white Mercedes-Benz delivery van shot through the intersection just ahead. The policeman driving the squad car slammed on the brakes. The driver of the van swerved left and turned into the street ahead of us.

We drove on, following the van now. After a hundred yards or so the van slowed down to a crawl. Then it stopped completely. The blinking hazard lights came on—the van driver was making a delivery.

The policeman behind the wheel brought the squad car to a halt twenty feet or so from the van's rear bumper. Cars were parked along both sides of the street. There wasn't room to get around the van.

The policeman behind the wheel hit the police siren. A short burst.

We waited.

The van didn't move.

The policeman said, "*Merde.*"

He hit the siren again. A longer burst.

The delivery van remained where it was.

The policeman looked into the rearview mirror.

He said, "*Merde encore.*"

I turned and looked too. A green Audi sedan driven by a dark-haired woman had just pulled up behind us. From her hand gestures it was clear that she wasn't happy about the traffic blockage either.

The policeman behind the wheel sighed. He opened the car door to get out. He was going to have a talk with one or the other of the drivers. Try to get things moving again.

The policeman was still climbing out of the patrol car when the rear doors of the delivery van burst open. Three men jumped down out of the back of the van. They were dressed in street clothes—blue jeans, heavy sweaters, tennis shoes. Perfectly ordinary clothing. Except for the black ski masks they wore to hide their faces.

The submachine gun in the hands of one of the men wasn't hidden. It was out in plain sight.

So were the automatic pistols held by the other two.

There was a half second where exactly nothing happened. A half second that felt like a lifetime. The men in front of us in the street studied us through the eyeholes in their woolen masks. The guns pointed at the windshield of the police car remained silent. The driver of the police car stood behind the open car door, one hand gripping the top edge of the door frame, almost casual in his pose. The policewoman reached out to grip the dashboard as she peered out of the windshield.

Then, like a cloud burst, the rattle and crack of small arms fire filled the street.

The driver caught it first. He was lifted up and spun around and tossed backwards onto the street like an empty paper cup in a hard wind. The windshield disappeared just as I leaned forward to duck my head. Flying glass rolled over me. The policewoman in the front passenger seat was hit as she tried to unholster her pistol. She came to rest lying across the gear shift console.

The guns fell silent.

I kept my head down. Somehow I'd avoided being shot. The policeman next to me in the back seat had slumped down, his knees pushing against the back of the front passenger seat. He was absolutely still. I realized that he hadn't returned fire even though he held his pistol in his right hand. His eyes were open. He was covered by a fair amount of blood.

I raised my head. Only an inch or two.

I glanced to my left.

The door window was a cobweb of cracks and small holes. One of the gunmen had reached the side of the car and was now pulling on the door handle.

He was here to deliver the *coup de grace*.

I couldn't move. I was terrified. The door opened roughly. Particles of glass from the shattered window fell on me. I had reached the end of my life. I was now looking at the last things I would ever see on this earth. The shattered window. The gunman in his woolen mask. An automatic pistol barrel. And then darkness.

The gunman let go of the door.

He looked at me. He took aim with the pistol.

And then he was shot squarely in the chest.

The gunman stumbled backwards. He fell against a parked car. He slid to the ground with his legs splayed in front of him. His chin came to rest on his chest. Before I had a chance to make sense of what I had just seen the policeman next to me raised his legs and pushed me out of the car with his feet.

I fell into the street. The air smelled of burned gunpowder and the diesel fuel spilling from the Peugeot's ruptured tank. I got to my hands and knees and glanced back at the police car just as gunfire kicked up again. The policeman was firing now. One round after another. Aiming between the front

4

seats at the van in front of the police car.

He was making no effort to escape.

I didn't try to help him. Thoughts of prying the gun free from the hand of the wounded gunman and making a heroic last ditch stand did not enter my mind. All I wanted was a place where I would be safe from the gunfire. I scrambled on my hands and knees toward a narrow space between two cars parked at the curb. I crawled between the cars and threw myself onto the sidewalk.

I raised myself to my knees. I was out of the line of fire. I glanced back one last time. The policeman was still in the back seat. His ammunition clip was empty now and he was trying to pull a fresh clip from a pouch on his pistol belt.

He didn't have time.

A burst of machine gun fire pushed his head and shoulders through what was left of the Peugeot's rear window.

A half a second later one of the gunmen stumbled around the front of the parked car beside me. He held his machine gun loosely at his side. He seemed disoriented. He staggered forward a few feet. Then dropped to his knees and sat back on his haunches.

One side of his ski mask was moist with blood and there was blood in his eyes. He didn't realize that I was there and he let the machine gun hang loose from the sling around his neck as he reached up and pulled the cap off. The right side of his head was covered in blood. He balled up the cap and tried to wipe the blood from his eyes, using the cap and then his bare hand.

Then he saw me. And I recognized him. It was the stout man with the tightly drawn face and the flattened nose. The man who had stepped inside the Café Alcazar the night before, while I was seated at the bar.

But none of that mattered now. In total panic I clambered to my feet. I saw a passageway between two buildings to my left, only a few yards ahead. The bloodied gunman was still on his knees trying to get the barrel of his machine gun up and pointed at me.

I rushed forward and kicked the gunman with every ounce of strength that I had. I aimed for his bloody head but my aim was bad. My foot landed a glancing blow against his shoulder instead. He lost his grip on the machine gun as the blow knocked him back.

But I knew it hadn't done him any damage.

As I ran past him a pistol shot rang out. There was still one other gunman left. I heard the man behind me shouting to his colleague. In the same instant a short burst of machine gun fire shattered a store window ahead of me.

I ducked into the passageway and kept running.

It was a narrow passageway between the stone walls of two buildings. I could see a patch of light at the end of it. I had no idea what lay beyond. Perhaps it led to the next street over. Or perhaps it led to a courtyard surrounded by a tall wall that I could never hope to scale before one of the gunmen appeared and shot me in the back.

But these questions were academic.

The passageway was my only hope.

2

My name is Richard Slade.

Richard Slade, of St. Louis, Missouri. Forty-three years old. Divorced, no children. No other family, to speak of. I earned a graduate degree in business administration from Washington University in St. Louis, and spent the next twenty years as a salesman for Thorssen Chemical, a Missouri-based firm that manufactures agricultural pesticides.

I can say with a certain authority that, contrary to common wisdom, pesticides breed pests. Pests like the Bulgarian government officials who demand a kickback every time I enter their airspace. Pests like the Italian farm collectives who use pesticides to scorch the earth down to bare rock, then demand compensation for the destroyed crops and lost productivity. Pests like the Egyptians who won't buy anything until their entire family has had the opportunity to render a verdict on my character, personal integrity, marriage prospects, and the state of my teeth.

But I learned how to survive in the pesticide trade.

I wasn't born yesterday.

But I'm not always smart.

I flew into Budapest, Hungary on business three weeks ago. I had already spent two weeks in Berlin and Prague, and Budapest was my last stop. If I'd been smart I would've finished my business in Budapest and gone directly home to St. Louis, rather than stopping in Nice.

A light rain was falling as my flight landed at Nice-Cote D'Azur International Airport. I'd decided on the spur of the moment to stop in Nice to look up an old friend. He was spending the winter months on the Cote D'Azur. A little vacation place, in Antibes.

It would be good to see him again.

I took a taxi to my hotel. Nice looked strangely unfamiliar under the gray skies and rain. The shops and cafes along the Promenade Des Anglais stood empty. The beach was deserted and the Mediterranean Sea looked darker and dirtier than I recalled from previous visits. I checked into the Hotel Negresco in the late afternoon. I had called my friend, Septimus Morgan, once from Budapest before I'd left and once again at the airport in Nice when I arrived. I hadn't reached him but I'd left messages. Now the hotel clerk handed me a cryptic phone message written on yellow notepaper.

It read: *Café Alcazar—19h.*

The caller hadn't left a name or number but I thought nothing of that. It could only be from Morgan. No one else knew I was here.

I wondered why he hadn't called my cell phone, but that was all I wondered.

I settled into my room. At half past six I went downstairs and stepped outside. The rain had subsided into a mist. The café was located on the Rue de Catelet, a few streets behind and to the east of the Negresco. It was a small, quiet place, clean and well-lighted.

A zinc-surfaced bar stood at one end. I sat down at the bar and ordered a glass of Beaujolais.

It was seven-thirty. Morgan was late. I picked up the *carte de maison* when a woman stepped into the cafe.

She paused just inside the door to look around.

Then she approached the bar and sat down on the bar stool next to mine.

She was maybe thirty years old. Brown eyes. Sun-tanned complexion. She wore a lightweight green raincoat that had a plastic sheen to it. Her blonde hair was curled into a mass of small rings. I was sure it was a wig.

There were several empty seats at the bar, but she chose to sit next to me. My first thought was that she was a prostitute. I waited for her to ask me if I was looking for a friend for the evening, or something along those lines.

The woman leaned in close.

She said, in British-accented English, "I'd walk a mile for a Camel."

"Excuse me?"

"A Camel cigarette. I'd walk a mile for one."

As a chat-up line it was novel. I smiled. "All right."

"Do you have a cigarette?"

"As it happens, I do not."

"Are you sure?"

Just then I looked down and stopped smiling.

Both of the woman's hands rested below the edge of the bar counter. One of her hands was empty. In the other she held a nickel-plated pistol with a short barrel. Just small enough to be easily carried in the pocket of a lightweight raincoat with a plastic sheen.

The muzzle was pressed into my side.

The bartender stood at the far end of the bar, talking to a gray-bearded man eating soup. I wondered if I should shout for help. With the barrel of a gun poking me in a kidney, that course of action didn't have a lot to recommend it. I looked again at the woman. She glanced past me, in the direction of the café's front door. There was a flicker of apprehension in her eyes. But when her eyes returned to me they looked hard and determined.

The woman said, "I'll ask you once more."

I said, "You've got your wires crossed."

She leaned in close again. Almost whispering in my ear. "Give it to me."

The earnest words sounded silly. I wondered if this was a practical joke. Had Morgan put the woman up to this? Perhaps the pistol shot nothing but a stream of water. I hazarded a look over my shoulder. Thinking I might see Morgan, laughing and pointing at me from across the room.

But Morgan wasn't there.

"You've made a mistake," I said now. I shook my head. "I'm sorry but I can't help you."

She pressed the pistol harder into my side. "Then we'll settle our business later."

"We don't have 'business.'"

"You'd better watch yourself."

The pressure from the muzzle of the gun in my side disappeared. The woman slipped the pistol back into her pocket but the bulge in her raincoat told me that the barrel was still pointed at me. She slid herself off the stool. She glanced once more at the front door and then walked quickly toward the back of the café. The heels of her boots hitting the tiled floor made a pick-pock sound.

The woman disappeared into a hallway that led to the kitchen. A SORTIE sign told me there was also an exit back there.

The entire exchange had taken three minutes at most. I had no idea what to make of it. I drank down the rest of my wine. I studied the hallway the woman had disappeared into.

She didn't reappear.

I didn't expect her to.

I wondered what she'd been after. And what the reference to cigarettes meant. I turned to study the front door. The door was closed. A single streetlight lit the sidewalk outside.

The bartender appeared. He thrust his chin at my empty wine glass.

"*Encore?*"

"*Oui.*"

I ran my hand down my sport coat to smooth the pocket flap where the woman had pushed the pistol into my side. I felt something in the pocket and slid my hand inside. My fingers came into contact with a small rectangle of metal.

I pulled it out.

It was a USB flash drive. A little smaller than a child's schoolroom eraser. A tiny imprint bore the brand name— POLARIS. It appeared to be an entirely standard flash drive in every respect.

But it wasn't mine.

I'd never seen it before.

By an odd coincidence, I did have a flash drive with me that night. It was tucked away in my inside coat pocket. It contained a file that I intended to give to Morgan. I checked my inside pocket. My flash drive was still there.

This new wrinkle perplexed me even more.

I tucked the other flash drive back into the pocket where I'd found it. I'd take a look at the contents when I got back to the hotel. Perhaps there was something on it that would tell me what the woman had truly wanted.

I gave Morgan another half hour. He didn't turn up. I called his cell phone number from the café but there was still no answer. I'd lost interest in eating and decided to leave. If Morgan showed up later, he'd just have to come around to the Negresco and meet me there.

I was settling my check when I heard the front door open.

A man stepped inside.

He was a stout man wearing a gray wool overcoat that looked too heavy for the weather. A tan racing cap with a wide bill was pulled low over his forehead.

The man stood just inside the door. His gaze fell on me. The man's nose was flat and crooked and his skin looked tightly stretched across the contours of his face. His hands were tucked deeply into his overcoat pockets. His dark eyes moved on, taking in the bartender, the two other customers at the bar, then back to the customers seated at the tables, where he'd first looked.

After a moment he turned slowly and left.

The door rattled as he closed it behind him.

I made no connection between the woman with the pistol and the man who had just come in. Perhaps I should've, but I didn't. I finished the last of my wine and got up. Buttoned my sport coat. Turned up the collar.

I left the café.

The dimly-lit street was empty. I started off toward the

Negresco. My mind raced around sharp corners. The woman with the pistol had left the flash drive in my pocket without getting anything in return. *We'll settle our business later*, she'd said. Would I be seeing her again? I couldn't see how. She didn't know me from a hole in the head. Who I was, or where I was staying.

I heard the sound of footsteps.

Somewhere behind me hard-soled shoes hit the gritty sidewalk with deliberation. Not a woman's high heels—it was a man walking, I was sure.

I turned quickly. The footsteps stopped. I waited. I couldn't see much of anything in the misty darkness. After a minute I told myself it was nothing. I was letting my imagination get the best of me.

I started off again. But walking a little faster now, while a thousand tiny needles crawled up my spine and across my scalp.

3

I took a circuitous route back to my hotel from the Café Alcazar that night. On the off chance that someone was following me. The streets remained silent but the rain returned. I had neglected to bring my umbrella and I was drenched by the time I reached the Negresco.

Returning to my hotel room I took a hot shower and changed into dry clothes. I ordered a double gin and tonic from room service and sat down to study the flash drive that the woman had dropped into my coat pocket.

The name on the device—POLARIS—stared back at me. It meant nothing to me. I noticed something else written on the face of the flash drive that I hadn't noticed before. A manufacturer's code—EN2606. But again, it told me nothing.

My gin and tonic was delivered by a stooped man in a red bellhop's jacket. When he'd gone I sat down at the desk and drank down half of the cocktail right off. I pulled my laptop from its traveling case and opened it up. Then I uncapped the flash drive and inserted it into the port on my computer.

When I tried to open the contents of the flash drive I came up against a gray dialogue box that asked me for a password.

I typed in words at random for a few minutes but INVALID PASSWORD continued to appear in the dialogue box. I wasn't too surprised. I tried a few alternate methods to get past the password screen but it was hopeless. Finally I shut down the computer. My little detective fantasy had gone flat. I finished my gin and tonic and ordered another. I finished the second one standing at the window. It was ten o'clock now and the rain had slackened off again. I noticed a small bistro across the street. Sitting in a warm bistro drinking with other strangers seemed preferable to sitting in a hotel room drinking alone.

The gin had limbered me up.

I tried calling Morgan once more. Still no answer. I left another message, told him that if he showed up tonight and I wasn't at the hotel, I'd be across the street at the bistro.

I was ready to leave when I realized that I might need some Euros. I had no Euros in my wallet and I'd given the bartender at the café the last of my coins, but I still had three hundred Euros in folding money tucked away for an emergency.

I took off my left shoe. It was a leather boat shoe and the inside of the sole underneath the footpad was composed of a plastic grid-like foundation. Being a reasonably paranoid traveler I had cut out a piece of the grid work to create a compartment just big enough to carry a tight roll of reserve cash. I pried out the roll of notes, removed the plastic wrap they were bound up in.

I dropped my own flash drive into my pocket, in case Morgan finally turned up, and left my room.

Riding the elevator down to the lobby I pondered the question of the password again. What were the obvious passwords? A person's name, of course. A street address or birth date. Perhaps the name of a loved one or a pet. I wondered idly what a proper name was for a bewigged Englishwoman of thirty or so. 'Penelope' sounded inexorably English. Her friends would call her 'Penny.' And if she made a habit of waving pistols around in cafés she would be called 'Bad Penny.'

The elevator doors slid open. I stepped out and followed the hallway to the hotel lobby. The front desk came into view. The night clerk stood behind it, talking to a man leaning against the other side of the counter. A thin man wearing a windbreaker over a bulky brown sweater. The man's face was dark and heavily-lined.

As I came closer, the clerk gave the other man a knowing look and nodded in my direction. The other man turned. He straightened up slowly as he watched me approach. He squared his shoulders.

Then he stepped in front of me.

"Excuse me, my friend," the man said, in English. "May I have a word with you?"

I had no idea who this man was. But I didn't like the look of him. All I wanted was to walk across the street and scare up another drink. I'd had enough oddball palaver for one night.

I said, "I'm on my way out."

"You have a moment."

"Some other time."

I started to step around the man.

He reached out to grab me.

I pushed him aside, maybe a little too hard. He fell backwards and hit the counter behind him, off-balance. One arm slid along the countertop a few feet as he tried to keep himself upright.

My instincts told me to get out of there. I moved fast toward the bank of glass doors. I was too scared to look back. I pushed one of the doors open and broke into a run. I was outside now. I'd reached the sidewalk before I realized that two men were rushing toward me from out of the shadows.

I darted to the right on the sidewalk just as one of the men tried to tackle me. He lost his hold on me but in the process I lost my balance. I fell head first into the rear door of a car that was parked at the curb.

I hit the ground on my hands and knees.

A knife-sharp pain shot down my back.

The two men came up on either side of me. It was only then that I noticed that they wore the dark blue fatigue uniforms of the municipal police. The two policemen grabbed me by the collar of my shirt and the waist of my pants. I thought they were helping me to my feet. They weren't. When they had a firm grip on me they slammed my head into the already dented police car door a second time. Just to make sure they had my full attention.

4

I wrote poetry in college.

But don't get the wrong idea.

I didn't have a precious artistic soul that was shouting to be heard above the teeming masses. Nothing like that. It was simply that I was curious about how poems were put together.

I didn't write any great poems, but they were good enough that my classmate and friend, Septimus Morgan, helped me get them published in the college magazine.

Which, as it happened, he was the editor of.

Then I left college and set aside poetry and went out into the world to become a success. I fell into sales work—the penultimate refuge of a scoundrel, I was told. At the age of forty I found that I was nothing more than a traveling salesman. No different than the desperate men in cardboard suits who used to sell vacuum cleaners and encyclopedias door-to-door.

The grinding slavery and dissimulation of a salesman's life had no value. I wanted something more.

I didn't know what, but I wanted it.

I had kept in touch with Morgan after college. He went

on to work as a reporter for the New York Times, then Newsweek magazine. When he married his English bride, Cordelia, he moved to the Cotswolds and pursued journalism on a freelance basis. The last time I'd seen Morgan was two years ago. He'd just purchased the holiday apartment in Antibes. I was in Paris on business and I drove down to Antibes for a visit.

At a local restaurant, I hinted at my existential disenchantment. Morgan picked up on it right away. In his view the answer to my malaise was to find a hobby. Why not write a novel? It might be just the thing, he said.

A novel? I gave it a moment's thought. I remarked idly that the only novel I had read recently was a slapdash thriller about a man and a woman who dodged bullets and good sense for two hundred pages, before disappearing into an ambiguous ending.

Morgan threw his hands up. "Great. Do the same thing."

"Someone's already done it."

"There's only ever been one plot, Richard—'Things are not what they seem.'"

I took Morgan's suggestion, more or less. Instead of a novel I decided to return to poetry. I sat up nights scratching away at tiny verses. Soon I had two or three good ones, then two or three more. Over time I refined these poems into a thin collection.

All I needed now was help in getting the manuscript published. The obvious candidate was Morgan. I tried to contact him in England before I left the States. It was Cordelia who told me that he'd gone to the Antibes apartment to finish up some writing assignments of his own. He wasn't expected back until early December.

She gave me his cell phone number but I put off calling him. Suddenly I was having second thoughts about the collection. It wasn't until I finished my work in Budapest that I decided to drop in on Morgan in Antibes. A couple of days in Antibes would be relaxing, whatever else transpired—or didn't.

I thought of all this as I sat alone and tired and angry in a cold bare room. Waiting for someone to explain to me why I had been picked up by the Nice municipal police at the Negresco. My passport had been taken from me, but nothing else. I tried again to reach Morgan on my cell phone.

I needed his assistance more than ever.

During the ride to the station, the plainclothes detective—the dark thin man I'd encountered at the Negresco's front desk—sat next to me in the back of the police car, with the two uniformed policemen up front. He turned on the dome light and studied my passport.

Then he said, apropos of nothing, "Mister Slade, you are not among friends. You might disappear for a very long time. While we piece together why it is, exactly, that you are here in Nice."

I assumed that the detective's interest in me had something to do with the Englishwoman at the café, but at the police station the detective disappeared without explaining a thing. The two uniformed policemen who escorted me to an upstairs room knew nothing either. One of them pushed me down into a plastic chair—"*Assis-toi.*" When they departed they locked the door behind them.

My head hurt from the beating it had taken against the car door, but I was still in one piece. I hadn't been restrained. My wrists were not handcuffed. I took that as a good sign and I tried to stay calm. I had done nothing wrong. A woman had pulled a pistol on me in an unfamiliar café, for reasons that weren't at all clear. Granted, it was a strange turn of events. But in no way did it make me culpable in anything. In parts of St. Louis it would be rated as an average night out.

The plastic chair sat in front of a wooden desk. Behind the desk was another plastic chair. Across the room was a gray metal locker. The locker door hung open. It was empty. I got up and walked around the room. Through a dirty window I could see police vehicles parked in the courtyard below.

I had no idea what part of Nice I was in.

I was alone in the room for quite some time. I called Morgan's phone number again and again. I got no answer but I left three or four detailed messages—each one more shrill than the last. After a half-hour it became clear that the cell phone battery was dying. I put the phone away. I was back standing at the window when I heard the door open.

I turned.

A tall man with a drooping moustache and a bald head stood in the doorway. He held a brown accordion file in his hand.

"Good evening, Mister Slade," the man said, in English. "Return to your seat, please."

"I want to know why I'm here."

"Be patient, Mister Slade."

"Am I under arrest?"

"Not at the moment."

"Then I can leave."

"No, you cannot. Now sit down."

"Who are you?"

The man stepped farther into the room. "I am Inspector

21

Brissac. I represent the *Police Nationale*. It seems there is a small matter that perhaps you can help us with."

I said, "I want to know my rights."

The inspector nodded his head. His bare scalp reflected the harsh light from the overhead bulb rather well. He said, "Right now you've got the right to take a seat. If you choose to remain standing, then you have the right to have your legs kicked out from under you and your neck shackled to that chair. I think that about covers your rights."

The inspector stroked his moustache while he waited to see what my answer would be. There didn't seem to be anything to gain by arguing, so I returned to the plastic chair and sat down. The inspector took the seat behind the desk. Right then a uniformed cop hurried into the room. The cop closed the door hard and approached the desk and set the black laptop computer that he'd brought with him down. Then he frowned and rushed back out of the room. He returned a minute later with a plastic chair for himself.

The uniformed cop settled in with his computer. It hummed and burbled to life. Inspector Brissac removed my passport from the accordion file. He paged through it, not so interested.

"So," Brissac said. "You are Richard Slade. And you entered France just today?"

"This afternoon."

"At Nice-Cote D'Azur Airport."

"That would be the one."

While Brissac asked the questions, the other cop tried to transcribe the interview. He typed with two fingers. There were long pauses while Brissac waited for the other cop to catch up.

22

After ten minutes Brissac still had not told me why I was here, and I wasn't going to bring up the subject of the Englishwoman myself. I glanced at my watch. It was nearly two o'clock in the morning.

I said, "Can we get to the point?"

Brissac raised his eyebrows. Bemused furrows of skin stretched across his forehead. He leaned forward in his chair and balled his hands into fists and set them down firmly on the desk. "Mister Slade, let me remind you. This is a police station. I am conducting a police investigation."

"I'm not under arrest."

"So it is this question of arrest that still troubles you," Brissac said. "Let me explain a little something. Under French law I can hold you here for forty-eight hours without charging you with a crime. And I don't have to give you access to a lawyer until twenty hours have elapsed. So you have at your disposal a great deal of time to sit here with me and enjoy my captivating personal qualities. That is, unless I decide to have you charged. In which case you can set aside any thoughts of returning to the United States this year. At the very least."

"Charge me with what?"

Brissac removed his fists from the desk.

He navigated a new tack.

"Tell me about the woman you met at the café tonight," he said. "Where you had your drink."

So Brissac knew about the woman. Now we were getting somewhere. I told Brissac everything that I dared to. I left out only the fact that the woman had pressed a pistol into my side. And that she left a flash drive in my pocket. Those two facts were just the sort of thing that might make Brissac think that he needed to keep me here. I was taking a risk by not telling him, but it seemed like a small risk. I just wanted to get this over with and get back to my hotel.

Brissac nodded along as I talked. Then he said, "Have you met her before? Or seen her anywhere?"

"I don't even know her name. I assumed she was a Brit."

"She asked you for a cigarette. But then she left. In a hurry. Out of the back of the cafe."

"Go figure."

"Excuse me?"

"*C'est la vie.*"

"What else did the woman tell you at the café?"

"Nothing."

"But she gave you something, isn't that right?"

I lied. "I don't believe so."

Brissac paused while the second officer caught up. After a moment the sound of typing stopped. Brissac said, "The bartender at the café said that he saw you puzzling over something in your hand after the woman left. Did the woman give you something?"

I reassessed my situation. I decided not to deny that I knew about the flash drive. But I downplayed it.

"She didn't give me anything," I said. "But after she left I noticed a flash drive on the counter, where she had been sitting. You know, a memory stick. It was partly hidden under the wine list. I picked it up and took it with me. I don't know who it belonged to. I suppose it could have been hers."

"Why did you take it?" Brissac said. "Why did you not give it to the bartender? In case the owner returned for it."

"It didn't seem important. And I had a use for a spare flash drive myself."

Brissac sat back. He thought about my answers. Then he

reached down and pulled a photograph out of the accordion file on the desk.

He said, "You walked home from the café tonight, is that right, Mister Slade? You did not take a taxi?"

"I walked."

Brissac tossed the photograph across the desk.

It was a grainy black and white photo. A narrow street at night. It looked like it might've come from a closed circuit traffic camera. There were some reflections of light off what looked like trash cans, and a small car parked half on the sidewalk and half in the street. There was a blurry figure in the center of the frame, emerging from the shadows and stepping into the street.

Then I realized what I was looking at.

It was a picture of me. Taken as I walked back to the Negresco from the Café Alcazar.

"Do you recall walking along that street?" Brissac said.

"Not particularly. I'm not familiar with the streets in Nice. I don't live here, as I think we've already established."

"For my part, I have established that the woman you met in the café was a French national. She wore a green raincoat. You indicated that her name was Monika Robichaux."

"She didn't tell me her name."

"My mistake."

Another photograph emerged from the accordion file. Brissac gave this one a glance and then slid it across the desk. The color image had something shiny in the center of it, but it wasn't a pair of trash cans. It was a shiny green raincoat. The front of the coat lay open and inside the coat was a woman. She lay on the cobblestones. One arm flung over her head. Her blonde hair was in disarray and her face was partly hidden by the collar of the raincoat but it looked like the same woman I had encountered in the café.

Except that when I had seen her last, her eyes weren't cold and dead. And there hadn't been a large pool of blood under her head.

I stared at the picture.

Brissac watched me.

"Mister Slade, we found this woman only a few hours ago," Brissac said. "She is dead. The alley that she was found in is not far from the Hotel Negresco. In fact, it is an alley that connects with the street that you were photographed on at roughly the same time that this woman was killed. We found a pistol in the pocket of her raincoat. It was not fired. From this we have surmised, quite reasonably, that whoever killed her was someone she knew and was not afraid of. She would have used the pistol to defend herself otherwise.

"Mister Slade, tell me why you had to kill her."

My heart pounded. Blood pulsed in my ears. I couldn't tear my eyes away from the photograph.

I was in serious trouble.

There were more questions but I had no answers. Finally a third policeman entered the room. Brissac told me that we were finished, for the moment. He explained that we were in a municipal police station right now, but shortly I would be transported to the National Police provincial headquarters across town, where I would be questioned again. It would be Brissac who ultimately decided whether I should be placed under arrest.

I stared at Brissac. I watched his mouth move. I nodded along but I couldn't take in the import of what he was saying. Municipal police or National Police, what difference did it make? All I knew is that things looked bad for me. I had no doubt that I would be arrested. Charged. Thrown into a cell.

The third policeman placed his hand on my shoulder. It was time to go. I stood up.

Brissac told the third policeman to wait.

"I have almost forgotten." Brissac held out his hand. "Mister Slade, the computer device that you took from the bar—do you have it on your person?"

Somewhere within the deep fog that had fallen over my awareness I heard the question and made sense of the words. I nodded slowly. It seemed to take a great effort. I removed the flash drive from my pocket and dropped it into Brissac's open hand.

I was taken to a holding cell. The policeman escorting me didn't bother to close the cell door. I sat down on the cot, my elbows on my knees. I stared at the floor without seeing it. All I could see was the dead woman lying in the alley.

Slowly my thoughts shifted. I realized that I had been less than forthright with Brissac. Partly out of a natural contrariness, and partly to keep myself from getting too involved in a police matter. But now that the police matter had revealed itself to be murder—well, there were things that I needed to discuss, for the record. The pistol the woman had drawn on me. Her comment that we'd settle our business later. The sound of footsteps behind me in the darkness and my fear of being followed from the café. I needed to tell Brissac all of it. Make a clean breast of things. It wasn't too late. Surely Brissac would understand. I had left a few things out of my story only because I was scared.

A policewoman appeared. She had brought me a cup of coffee. I told her I wanted to see Brissac. She wasn't interested.

She handed me the cup and shrugged as she left. I drank some of the coffee. I set it aside and poked my head out of the holding cell. A policeman sitting at a desk down the hall saw me and motioned for me to get back inside.

"I must see Inspector Brissac," I said.

The policeman got up from his chair. He unhooked a ring of keys from his belt as he came down the hallway toward me. When he reached my cell I explained to him that it was imperative that I speak to Brissac. I had information that Brissac desperately needed.

The policeman nodded. He said he understood perfectly. He smiled.

Then he placed his hand on my chest and pushed me back into the cell and pulled the door closed. With a rattling of keys he locked it and walked away.

5

I felt a drop of water hit my face.

At least it wasn't blood.

I sat in a broken-down barn at the edge of an orchard. Somewhere on the outskirts of Nice. It was raining. The rainwater dripped down on me through the holes in the roof. The front of the barn was wide open. From where I sat I could see, perhaps a mile to the south, a section of the A8 highway.

It was still early morning. It was difficult to believe that only an hour ago masked gunmen had murdered the three French policemen escorting me across town, and had nearly killed me too.

Twenty or so yards from the barn was a narrow road. Across the road was a large field and beyond the field was a long three-story block of apartments. Lines of drying clothes hung from balcony railings and run-down cars were parked in rag-tag fashion at the rear of the building.

I remember all of this clearly. But what preceded it is hazy.

I recall running. Harder than I have ever run. Running down the passageway between the two buildings to make my escape from the gunmen who ambushed the police car. I heard shouting behind me. Were they chasing me? I didn't look back. Just as I reached the end of the passageway there was a single gunshot. The round ricocheted off the stone walls. Small chips of stone hit me in the face.

The passageway led to a patio. I seem to recall a wooden fence covered in ivy. The next thing I remember is running along a sidewalk. I knocked people aside as I ran. I ran like I had the hounds of hell on my trail. I ran until I thought my pounding heart would jump out of my chest. When I couldn't run any longer I walked and kept walking, I had no idea where.

Rain began to fall. When I could go no farther I hid myself in the first place that presented itself—the barn. I was wet and cold. I had tossed my sport coat aside somewhere. It was spotted with blood. My shirt was black and the blood stains on the front weren't as obvious.

I sat down on a wooden crate inside the barn. I closed my eyes. I breathed slowly and deeply to calm myself. I told myself to think things through rationally but it wasn't possible. I had been accused of committing one murder, had watched three more occur, and had almost been killed myself. The truth of it was, I was a dead man. The rain eased up after a while. I found a discarded paint can in a pile of trash outside. Rainwater had collected in the can. I took off one of my socks and dampened it and used it to wipe my face. Then I cleaned the blood from my hands. I pulled the sock back on my foot and tied my shoes and left the barn.

I shivered in the cold morning air as I walked down the winding lane in the direction I had come. I had just passed under the highway when I noticed a helicopter hovering in the sky to the east. I didn't know if it was a police helicopter or not but I turned and headed west, just in case.

Eventually I came upon a small clothing shop run by an East Indian man. The shop was just opening for business. I stepped inside and looked at myself in a mirror and wiped away a smear of blood on my chin. I looked around and found what I wanted. A bulky jacket with a warm lining and a large collar. As I paid for the purchase the turbaned man studied the dark stains on my shirt. If he had any inkling of what had caused them he kept it to himself.

I left the shop and put the jacket on and turned up the collar.

Now I needed to find help.

As I walked on, without any real idea of what I was looking for, I found myself thinking of St. Louis. My condo in town wasn't much of a place to live, but after I gave up the marriage gambit I didn't feel that I wanted much. I had a nice view of the back of an auto repair shop from my living room window. And there was Loretta, who I had taken to dinner before I left on this trip. I met her at a coffee house on Locust Street. We had both ordered the pumpkin-flavored latte and, striking up a conversation based on that piece of happenstance, we found that we had nothing at all in common except the feeling of being at loose ends. My life in St. Louis didn't amount to much these days. But right at that moment, walking the streets of Nice with blood on my clothes and three French policemen lying dead in a street behind me, I wished more than anything that I was back in the dreariness of St. Louis.

Dreariness sounded like heaven to me.

I reached a tree-covered square surrounded by stucco

31

buildings with window shutters painted in pastel colors.

I stepped inside a small bistro on the far side of the square. I walked to the bathroom and washed my face once again, with warm water and a paper towel. I worked more water through my hair and tidied up. Then I stepped out of the bathroom and walked up to the bar.

The bartender didn't seem keen on mixing drinks at nine o'clock in the morning. I ordered a gin and tonic. The only gin he had was strictly bottom shelf, maybe from under the sink, but I didn't complain. I changed a ten-Euro note into coins and stepped into the hallway that led to the bathroom. A pay phone hung on the wall. I took a long drink of the gin and tonic and paged through the phone book that rested on a small table. I found the number I wanted, dropped a few coins into the phone box, pressed the buttons.

A brisk female voice answered.

"I need to speak to the consul," I said.

"The consul isn't available at the moment. Would you like to leave a message?"

"It's urgent. I'm a United States citizen and I've run into a little trouble. I need to speak to someone right now."

There was a long pause. I heard noise on the other end of the line. It sounded like the woman was rearranging the items on her desk. Finally she said, "And your name?"

I gave it to her.

"What is the nature of your problem, Mister Slade?"

"I'd rather talk to someone in charge."

"I can't refer your call properly unless I know what the nature of your problem is."

"The French police have accused me of a murder that I didn't commit. And if that's not enough, I was also involved in a gun battle two hours ago in the center of town. Three men with masks and a machine gun attacked the police car I was riding in. The three policemen in the car with me were shot dead. I escaped. How does all of that grab you?"

Another long pause.

Then, "Can you hold?"

The female voice disappeared. It was replaced by a buoyant pop melody played by the consulate's phone system. I drank the last of the gin and tonic down. I was chewing the ice when the female voice returned. She explained that she was transferring my call to a consular official named Webb.

A moment later a man's voice came on the line.

"Seward Webb here."

I asked the man if the receptionist had given him the particulars of my problem. He said that she had. He also said that he'd had a little difficulty believing it. That is, until he found a breaking news bulletin on the website of a Nice television station. The bulletin recounted the gun battle in Nice. It also mentioned my name. Webb was studying the bulletin as we spoke.

"One thing though," Webb said.

"What's that?"

"It says here that you're dead."

"That's a mistake."

"How can I be sure? There are a lot of sick people out there."

"What's that supposed to mean?"

"Sick people who like to play sick practical jokes."

"Listen to me, Webb. Whatever is going on here, it's not a joke. Three policemen are dead. The bullets that killed them were real. Last night a woman was also murdered. She was real too." For good measure I rattled off my full name, date of birth, home address in St. Louis, Social Security number.

After a pause Webb said, "Only two policemen died."

"One of them survived?"

"It says here that he's in the hospital. Seriously injured, but he's not dead. But if you think I can protect you from the French police, you are grossly mistaken."

"I need someone to help me, Webb. Someone who can look out for my interests. I don't know what is happening here or why, but I'm being falsely accused of murder. And two hours ago three men I don't know tried to kill me. There must be something you can do to help."

"You should turn yourself in."

"I want you there to represent me."

"I'm not a lawyer."

"But you can help me find one. A good one."

"This is very irregular."

"Tell me about it."

"Mister Slade, I can't help you until you turn yourself in."

I knew Webb was right. I had run because I was scared. But I couldn't run any farther. The longer I tried to elude the police, the more suspicion would fall on me.

"I'll turn myself in," I said. "But I want to talk to you first. I want to explain my side of things and I want you to write it down. So that there is a record of what happened. I don't want to disappear into a French jail and never be heard from again. And I want to talk to a lawyer. That's the deal, Webb."

"I'll see what I can do."

"I want your word."

After a pause and a sharp intake of breath he said, "You have it. Now, where are you?"

6

I was born on April Fool's Day. For many of my younger years my mother told me that being born on April the first was a source of great luck. But I always associated my birthday with a song I used to hear on the radio. It spoke of being born under a bad sign. And having only bad luck, if I had any luck at all. What possibly could be good about being born on the official day of fools?

Of course, as I grew older, I came to realize that every day is the official day of fools.

Right then I wondered which one of us was the bigger fool—Seward Webb, for involving himself in my cause, or myself, for believing that he could help me. I wondered how far I could trust Webb. Based on our phone conversation I didn't think much of him. More than ever, I wished that I could reach Morgan. Maybe Webb could help me locate him.

Webb had said he'd meet me in the square in an hour. He'd come alone and we'd talk. I could explain to him the events of the last fifteen hours. Then we'd work out the particulars of my surrender to the *Police Nationale*.

The atmosphere inside the bistro was stifling. I walked

outside and looked around. It didn't seem wise to stand around in plain sight while I waited. Brissac had my passport. Soon my photograph would be all over the television and the Internet, if it wasn't already.

I needed to make myself scarce.

I crossed the square and stepped into a side street. I kept walking. Keeping to the quiet side streets. This part of Nice was slow to awaken and that was my good fortune. But somehow I managed to make a complete circle and after fifteen minutes I found myself back on the square.

Then I saw what I needed.

The buildings along the north side of the square were built against a hill. On the hillside was a road that rose diagonally. Halfway up the road stood a low stone wall with a pair of black wrought-iron gates set into it. Beyond the gates was what appeared to be a graveyard.

I walked across the square and behind the buildings on the north side. I started up the road. The concrete surface of the road had worn away in places to expose the cobblestones underneath. When I reached the cemetery I found that I could see the square below very well from this position.

I decided to stay right there.

I forced the latch on the gates up and entered. There were all manner of gravestones, and mausoleums with ornate roofs, and everything crowded together. I found a spot near the front that gave me a view of the road outside and the square down below and I took a seat on a large and formidable upright gravestone.

Once or twice a car passed on the hillside road, but mostly it was quiet. The waiting and the grounds of the cemetery around me brought my thoughts around to Septimus

Morgan again. I recalled a story he used to tell. His widower grandfather had died at his home in Topeka, Kansas, and Morgan's parents asked Morgan to make the six-hour drive from St. Louis to Topeka to pick up the ashes. Morgan duly picked up the ceramic urn in Topeka, but facing the long drive back to St. Louis Morgan also picked up, appropriately, a fifth of Old Grand-Dad bourbon. Somewhere around Boonville, Missouri the bourbon took hold and Morgan decided he'd better stop for a nap. At a highway rest stop the funerary urn somehow fell out of the car and grandfather's earthly remains spilled out among the pebbles of gravel in the parking lot.

To make matters worse, it had begun to rain.

There is no easy way to disassociate fine wet ash from gravel, but Morgan was able to return the urn to its proper weight and deliver it to his parents. And to this day they are none the wiser that the Morgan family crypt in St. Louis does not contain much in the way of Grandpa Morgan's remains. It does, however, contain the remains of numerous Chesterfields, Raleighs, Viceroys, and Winstons, pilfered from the ashcans at numerous rest stops on the highway between Booneville and St. Louis.

It was a good story.

Knowing Morgan, it might even be true.

Another car passed on the road. I studied the iron gates of the cemetery where I now sat. They reminded me of the bars of the jail cell at the police station. I had no doubt that I'd be spending more time in a French jail cell soon, even if Webb could intervene with the authorities on my behalf. How long would it take for the wheels of police procedure to grind out my fate? With two policemen dead and one in the hospital with grave injuries, the French police would take a dim view of my case, Webb or no Webb. Things weren't going to be pleasant for me but I surmised that I should feel grateful. I might've been killed in the ambush myself. I might've been laid out in the morgue right now. I heard again the rattle of machine gun fire. Why ambush a police car? I couldn't imagine how it had anything to do with me. I had been in the wrong place at the wrong time, that was all.

But no, that wasn't all. Because it had been the second time in twelve hours that I was in the wrong place, at the wrong time. And the second time that I had encountered the man with the taught features and flattened nose.

It was no coincidence.

I checked my watch. Webb had told me he'd be driving a green Volvo station wagon with diplomatic license plates. I couldn't make out a license plate down in the square from where I sat but I certainly hadn't seen a green station wagon.

I did see a Volkswagen sedan. It pulled into the square and parked near the bistro where I had used the phone. Two men in casual clothes got out. They walked across the street and into the square. Just looking around. After a minute they returned to the Volkswagen and climbed in. They sat there, waiting.

They worried me.

I left the graveyard. I walked across the road and stood at a concrete barrier that ran along the edge of a turnout. Two small trees on the other side of the barrier kept me out of plain sight from the men in the Volkswagen below. From the turnout I had a much better view of the neighborhood around the square. I saw a police patrol car rolling slowly along a side street. The patrol car pulled up and parked a hundred feet from where the side street opened up into the square. The occupants remained inside the car.

Then I heard the helicopter.

It was only a faint rumbling at first. A dark speck in the distance. But quickly the rumbling grew louder. The dark speck became a white helicopter with police markings. It was traveling straight toward the square.

It was then that I knew that Webb had lied to me. What was he afraid of? All I'd wanted was a chance to talk to him—a chance to explain myself to a neutral party. Before I turned myself in to the French police.

The son of a bitch had called the police himself.

The words of the detective who'd picked me up at the Hotel Negresco rang through my mind. *You are not among friends. You might disappear for a very long time.*

I had to get out of there.

I returned to the graveyard and took up a position behind a crypt near the stone wall. I was still wondering how to escape the net that was falling over me when I heard the high-pitched whine of a car traveling fast in low gear. It was coming up the hillside toward the graveyard.

The car came into view.

It wasn't a police car.

It was a late model Audi. It pulled into the turnout and stopped. The engine idled softly as a man climbed out of the driver's seat. Then a woman emerged from the other side of the car.

I saw the man's face clearly. The woman's face remained turned away. The lower portion of her dark hair was tucked under her coat so that her long straight hair looked like a scarf tied around her head.

The two of them stood at the barrier at the edge of the turnout. Looking down into the square. Looking up at the helicopter that was now hovering nearby. They stood there for a few minutes. Not moving and not saying much. The woman kept her hands tucked into the pockets of her overcoat. Then the man said something to her and she turned toward him and said something in return, and that was when I saw the woman's face.

After another minute the couple returned to the car. When they had driven off I made my way to the back of the graveyard and around to the far side of the hill. I climbed over a stone wall and walked quickly down a cobblestone street. My head swam with thoughts of the woman I had just seen.

Her name was Monika Robichaux.

And according to the French police, she was dead.

7

Ten hours later I was riding in the cab of a Scania transport truck on a rain-slick highway at night.

The man behind the wheel had dark Mediterranean features. Two narrow scars ran horizontally across his nose. He might have been Turkish or North African or Arab or a mixture of all three, I couldn't tell. His command of English and French wasn't entirely up to snuff.

"Weather is bad," he said. He took his eyes off the road long enough to give me a gap-toothed smile. His teeth were as brown as his skin. "Luck is for you." He pointed to his chest to indicate that he was the luck in question.

My own thoughts were miles away. The face of the woman that I had seen on the road outside of the graveyard was burned into my mind. I saw it with my eyes closed. I saw it with my eyes open. I saw it in the dark wet landscape that rolled past the truck windows. I had recognized her, even without the blonde wig. There was no doubt in my mind that she was the same woman. Which meant that the woman in the photograph that Inspector Brissac had shown me was someone else.

But why?

Why did the police believe that the woman I saw had been murdered, and why was she still walking the earth, and crossing my path once again?

I had no answers.

But no one likes to be pushed around, and it seemed that someone was pushing on me awfully hard, to suit their own purposes.

I had already resolved to push back, as best I could.

I thought again of the stout man with the flattened nose. I had never seen the man in my life before I encountered him at the café. And yet the second time we ran into each other he was determined to kill me, whatever the cost. What had I done? I recalled the message that was waiting for me when I arrived at the Hotel Negresco. I'd assumed at the time that it was from Morgan. Now I wondered. Had the message been intended for someone else? Had I gotten it by accident?

I needed to find Morgan. I needed to know whether or not he'd left that message.

More to the point, I needed help. Before I was ground up and spit out by the French judicial system.

After I had escaped the graveyard in Nice, I found myself in a neighborhood bordered by warehouses. I caught a taxi outside of a tabac. I asked the driver to take me to the Russian Cathedral, on the Avenue Nicolas II. There, to help cover my tracks, I jumped into a second taxi. I asked the new driver to take me down the coast to Antibes. He quoted me an outrageous price for the trip. He was surprised when I agreed to it.

But right then I wasn't thinking about cash.

As I saw it, I was running for my life.

Thirty minutes later I was standing within the ancient stone walls of *vieille* Antibes with much less in my wallet than I'd had before. I walked into the first souvenir shop I found and purchased a baseball cap. I wanted to hide my face as much as possible from the scrutiny of passers-by. I started to use my credit card to pay but caught myself and used more cash—the credit card would leave a trail.

I walked out to the stone battlements that overlooked the harbor. I tried to recall where exactly Morgan's holiday apartment was. I couldn't call him because I hadn't committed his phone number to memory. My cell phone's memory was as dead as the rest of it.

After forty-five minutes of searching I found what I was looking for. It was a three-story block of twelve apartments situated on a road that ran along the seaside. The building wasn't anything special but the front windows and the balconies looked out over the placid sea and the yachts moored offshore.

At the rear of the building I climbed the outdoor stairs to the third floor. The steps were strewn with potted plants in poses of decomposition. I wondered how Morgan would react when he saw me. He must've gotten the phone messages I'd left by now. And if he'd gone to the Negresco, the front desk staff no doubt would've told him about my abrupt exit from the arms of that august establishment.

But Morgan wouldn't be prepared for the tale I had to tell.

I found Morgan's door and knocked. After a few more knocks it became clear that there was no one at home. Suddenly I was gripped by the fear that Morgan was not here, hadn't been here, wasn't even in the south of France. Had he changed his plans?

I walked back down the stairs feeling desperate. On the ground floor I knocked on the door belonging to the building manager. A short gray-haired woman answered the door.

She studied me with suspicion.

"I'm looking for Septimus Morgan," I said. I pointed upward to indicate the top floor of the building in case it helped her understanding. "Do you know when he'll return?"

The woman shrugged her rounded shoulders. "He is not here."

"I'm a friend of his."

"Is that so."

I told a small lie. "He's expecting me."

"Then I'm surprised that he is not here." The rounded shoulders hunched up around her thick neck. She looked down at her hands. She scratched the palm of one hand with the index finger of the other. After a moment I wised up. The old woman was giving me the international sign for baksheesh. I pulled out my wallet and opened it. I handed her a five-Euro note and then another. She tucked the notes into the pocket of her tattered apron and sighed. "Monsieur Morgan has gone to Sète."

"When will he be back?"

"He is staying in Sète."

"Where in Sète?"

"A friend of his would know where he was staying in Sète, don't you think?"

I laid a ten-Euro note on her open palm. It disappeared into the apron pocket with the others. The woman cocked her head to one side and focused her gaze on a point well to the left of me. She said, "There is a small artist's studio above a restaurant called Le Poulet Ivre. On the Rue Navier.

You might find him there."

"Is there a phone number where I can reach him in Sète?"

The woman retreated into her sphinx-like silence. I only had twenty-Euro notes left in my wallet. I handed her one and asked for ten Euros change. She handed me the ten I had given her a moment ago, paused, then added one of the five-Euro notes that I had given her at first. I was getting an answer to my last question at half price. Then I found out why.

She said, "No, I am sorry. I do not have a phone number for Monsieur Morgan in Sète. Good luck to you."

The woman closed the door.

Sète was a good 200 miles from Antibes. On the other side of Marseille. I certainly didn't have enough cash for a taxi ride to Sète. And taking a crowded afternoon train seemed ill advised. Given that every cop in southern France must've been watching for me by now.

But I wasn't ready to give up on Morgan.

I pulled the cap farther down on my head and started walking north. Toward the highway.

I'd hitch a ride.

It was five o'clock. Vehicles on the road slid past me with their headlights on in the dusk. I walked for half an hour. As I approached the highway I came upon a brightly-lit gas station. A restaurant called the Café Veronika stood a little farther on. Among the vehicles parked outside of the café I noticed a white passenger van with British license plates and a red and blue streamer taped across the inside of the rear window.

I stepped inside the café.

The warm air in the dining room had fogged the windows.

The room was full of tables and people gathered around the tables and their chatter. It was a truck stop, French style. I heard the door swing shut behind me with a bang and a rattle and for a moment I was reminded of the roadside diners that my father and I used to visit while we traveled through the Ozark Mountains. The waitresses would welcome us in out of the cold and make us feel at home while the cooks poured the steaming hot gravy on the meatloaf they had just pulled from the oven. Maybe it wasn't really like that—memories from childhood are never very reliable. Still, I felt a pang of dismay that I might never feel the safety and comfort of a roadside diner in the wintery Missouri backwoods again.

The trip that I was engaged in now might turn out to be my last, if I wasn't careful.

A small bar stood at the back of the restaurant. Lined up at the bar were six men in their twenties or early thirties. They wore parkas and woolen hats in the same color scheme as the banner in the van outside. I stepped up to the bar and ordered a gin and tonic. The drink came and I paid for it. I noticed that the six men all held tall cans of English beer in their fists. The nearest of the six men turned and glanced at my drink, then at me.

He squinted one eye to get a better focus on my face.

He said, "How goes it, mate?"

"Could be better. How about you?"

"Tip top. Off to see the games then?"

"I was driving to Sète. But my car broke down. Some sort of timing chain issue."

"You're an American," said another of the men. The fluffy red ball at the top of his wool cap fell to one side as he leaned forward to look around his friend at me.

"That's right," I said.

The second one looked at the first one, then at me again. "And you've banged up your motor?"

"More or less."

The first one said to me, "Not such a bad place to hole up, is it? South of France and all that. The women run naked on the beaches. Wouldn't mind a bit of French pastry before we go home to our meat and two veg, if you follow my meaning."

The first Englishman nudged the second one with an elbow. They laughed.

"Where are you gentlemen from?" I said. Just trying to keep the conversation going. Work it around to what I wanted to know—which direction they were traveling in. Just then one of the men finished his beer, pushed the empty twenty-ounce can across the bar, and removed a fresh can from the bulk of his jacket. I noticed that the name emblazoned on the can of beer was Grunstead's Bitter. The café manager looked askance at the men but it was obvious that he didn't have the stomach to try to restrict the Englishmen's drinking to the beverages he sold on the premises.

I pressed on. "Are you heading east or west?"

The man next to me smacked his lips together. "We're going down to Marseille. Which might be west, now that I think of it." He explained that he and his friends were on their way to Marseille to cheer on Blackpool's finest in their football match against "the grotty French team" known as Olympique Marseille.

"Any chance of catching a ride?" I said. "My car won't be fixed for a day or two. I have friends in Marseille who'll put me up. But they don't have a car themselves."

This brought a frown from the Englishman next to me. He

nudged the man next to him again. "The Yank needs a ride."

In a flurry of nods, grunts, and belches the Grunstead's Bittermen decided that they would be honored to give me a lift.

With one condition.

The Bitterman next to me leaned in close.

He said, "We'll need provisions."

I took the café manager aside. He assured me with no small amount of sorrow and gesticulation that there wasn't a single can of English beer of any kind in his establishment. I negotiated for two cases of French Kronenbourg beer and hoped for the best. Maybe the Englishmen had already drunk so much that they wouldn't notice the difference between a heavy English bitter and a light French lager.

I paid for the beer and followed the Bittermen out. At the door I stepped past a man on his way inside. He gave me a piteous look that seemed to say that whatever we were up to, it would come to a bad end.

8

Marseille was 90 miles from Antibes. By the time the highway wound down toward the port city the first of the two cases of Kronenbourg was a fading memory.

The man I'd stood next to in the café had introduced himself as McBrain. The driver of the van was an out-of-work bricklayer named Mickey Wedge. He performed valiantly behind the wheel but even so, there were moments when I was sure that I'd made a horrible mistake. That turning myself in at the nearest police station and letting them do their worst was preferable to sliding off the highway at 75 miles per hour and coming to rest against a tree in a heap of twisted metal, empty beer cans, and broken Grunstead's Bittermen.

We reached the outskirts of Marseille and at my direction Mickey Wedge pulled into a highway service stop to let me out. Hands were shaken. Backs were slapped. Exclamations of profound drunken friendship were traded. I extricated myself from the well-wishing and climbed out of the van.

I watched the van pull shakily out of the service stop, then I walked past the gasoline pumps and stepped inside the transit café. The fluorescent lights seemed too bright. I knew that catching a ride from Antibes to Marseille had been the easy part of the journey. The A8 and A57 highways linked the two cities directly. The trip from Marseille to Sète was going to be trickier. Sète was a relatively small town. There wasn't a direct route to get me from here to there. I might have to catch a series of rides before I could reach the seaside where Sète was located.

But my luck continued to hold.

I had just paid for a bottle of juice when a man with Arabic features walked in. He had pulled up to the diesel pumps in a cargo truck that belonged to a supplier of fresh fish. The lettering on the long cargo box read TRÉSOR DE LA MER S.A. Underneath, in smaller script, was an address and a phone number.

The fish supplier was based in Sète.

The truck driver paid for a bottle of mineral water. He stepped over to one of the high-top tables. He pulled his cell phone out and tapped in a number and talked quietly into the phone while he drank his water. When he closed his cell phone I walked over to his table.

I explained to the man in halting French that my car had broken down. Was there any chance of catching a ride with him to Sète?

The man looked skeptical. To help persuade him I pulled out my wallet and opened it. My funds were getting low but there were enough notes in my wallet to catch his interest.

We agreed on a price.

The cab of the truck smelled of incense and spoiled fish. The man pulled the truck out onto the highway and introduced himself as Mahmoud. It suddenly occurred to me that

I'd seen the man before. Was he the man who had walked into the Café Veronika back in Antibes, as I was walking out with the Englishmen?

"Luck is for you," Mahmoud said. His English was tortured but he was determined to speak it. "Sète is not easy place. Is long time from Marseille." Mahmoud made a kind of swimming motion with his hand to indicate the circuitous nature of the road to Sète. "Much twistings."

For the first few miles we remained on the main highway. Then Mahmoud turned onto a long series of dark secondary roads. Mahmoud kept the engine revved up and was quite calm as he sped through turns in the wrong lane, while the radio played Arabic music full of wailing voices and drums.

We had been driving for close to an hour and had just passed through the village of Villeneuve-lès-Maguelone when Mahmoud all of a sudden swerved toward the shoulder of the road. He pulled onto the loose gravel and hit the brakes. We came to a stop near a copse of tall trees. Mahmoud engaged the parking brake but left the engine idling.

"What's the matter?" I said.

"Make pizz," he said.

Mahmoud jumped down out of the cab and walked around to the back of the truck. A few minutes later he returned. As he climbed back into the cab of the truck I noticed that he had his cell phone in his hand. He'd called someone to chat while he relieved his bladder.

We drove on in silence. The road became darker and narrower. Twenty minutes later the engine began to sputter. Mahmoud gave me a concerned look. He made a big show of pumping the accelerator pedal and working the clutch and shifting gears but the sputtering continued and the truck slowed. We rounded a long curve. Ahead was a wide turnout that was lit by a roadside light pole. I saw a dark sedan parked in the turnout. The truck began to slow even more.

As the truck rolled into the turnout Mahmoud flashed the headlights on and off.

That's when I knew I was in trouble.

The truck was still rolling when I pushed open the passenger door. I was going to run. There was a vast darkness out there and I could run and keep running and hopefully lose myself in that darkness. I didn't know what Mahmoud or his friends in the sedan had in mind and I wasn't going to hang around to find out. I had one leg out and was ready to jump down to the ground when Mahmoud hit the brakes hard. I was thrown forward. My arms and head hit the dashboard. My legs tangled up under me. I was struggling to right myself and get out of the truck when I glanced at Mahmoud.

I stopped struggling.

Mahmoud held a fish knife in his hands. The shiny metal of the blade reflected the soft green and red lights from the dashboard. The tip of the blade was a few inches from my neck. Mahmoud smiled.

"Luck is *kaput*," he said.

9

I stared at the knife. Mahmoud smiled some more. I was being robbed. I pulled out my wallet slowly and tried to hand it to him. He shook his head. He only wanted the money. I opened the wallet and removed the Euro notes and handed them over.

Mahmoud stuffed the notes into his shirt pocket.

Two men climbed out of the Audi sedan parked in front of us in the turnout. They approached the truck. The passenger-side door hung ajar and one of the men grabbed it and opened it fully. The other one told me in French to get out. One of the men looked like an Arab. The other was fair-complexioned and spoke French like a Frenchman, as near as I could tell.

The Frenchman waved an automatic pistol around.

There was no point in putting up a fight.

The Arab threw me up against the cab of the truck and patted me down for weapons. When he finished, he removed a small electronic device the size of a pack of cigarettes from his pocket. Keeping the device a foot or so from my body he waved it up and down in front of me and then turned me around and waved the device around some more. I wasn't sure what the device was, but it occurred to me that perhaps he was looking for some sort of homing beacon or electronic signal that would give away my position to a third party. But that led to the question of what they might be worried about. Did they know who I was? If they did, then they also knew that I was on the run from the French police. I'd be the last person with a homing signal attached to their body.

But perhaps I was wrong about the device. Maybe they were just checking me for lice.

The Arab seemed satisfied and returned the device to his pocket. For no good reason that I could see he pulled the cap off my head and sent it sailing out into the darkness. Then the Frenchman pushed me forward. I was tossed into the back of the sedan. The other two climbed in on either side of me.

I heard Mahmoud laughing in the darkness. Then the car doors slammed shut.

The tires squealed and we bolted out of the turnout and sped off down the dark road. The driver was silent. The Arab on my left looked bored. The Frenchman kept the pistol pointed loosely at my right kidney.

"Where are we going?" I said. My voice sounded small. The Arab grunted and shifted his position on the seat. The Frenchman said, in perfect American-accented English, "Just relax and enjoy the ride."

"I'd enjoy it more if I knew what this was about."

"So would we."

I puzzled over that remark.

I said, "Where did you learn your English?"

"I used to live in New Jersey."

"You don't say."

"I worked for a dog food company in Newark. Until they fired me. They told me that my work didn't meet the high standards of their dog food. So I came home to Sète. And now I'm the head chef in a seafood restaurant. And you know something? No one complains about my cooking. Not once."

"This must be your night off then."

"I do the occasional odd job."

Ten minutes later the headlights illuminated a road sign that indicated we had just entered the town of Sète. The road curled through a stand of tall trees and then followed railroad tracks around a hill. Who had sent these men out to capture me? And by what coincidence did they bring me to the very place that I was trying to get to?

We rode along a well-lit street lined with shops and restaurants on one side and a canal on the other. I heard music from a nightclub and the beeping horns of motor scooters. We crossed a stone bridge. We were near the harbor and I caught glimpses between the old buildings of the lights of boats lying at anchor. The driver had rolled his window part of the way down and the air from outside was filled with pungent sea smells.

We entered a side street and pulled up in front of a large garage door. After a moment the door slowly rose and the car slipped into the darkness inside. A row of naked light bulbs hanging from the ceiling came on as soon as the door slid back down.

We were in a large garage with a high ceiling. The walls were bare rubble stone and the floor was smooth cement. A truck was parked at one end of the garage and beyond it I could see a small white door. The Arab and the Frenchman got out and ordered me to do the same. The driver stayed seated behind the wheel with the engine running.

"Come along," the Frenchman said.

The Arab took the lead as we walked toward the white door. The Frenchman kept his pistol handy as he brought up the rear. The Arab opened the door and we filed through the doorway and into a long hallway. White walls. White linoleum floor. White ceiling. Bright fluorescent lights. At the end of the hallway stood another white door.

I wasn't quite prepared for what lay beyond.

We had stepped into the lobby of a hotel. There was a registration counter to the right. Keys hung from hooks over the wooden boxes on the wall behind the counter. On the other side of the lobby a grand staircase with an ornate wooden balustrade led upstairs. A marble pilaster stood in the center of the lobby and behind us on the left was an elevator and straight ahead were a pair of pebbled glass doors.

Presumably the front doors of the hotel.

Leading to the street outside.

"The doors are locked," the Frenchman said. "In case you were wondering. Even if you could get through them you wouldn't make it far. Half the people in Sète work for El-Kef. Even some of the police."

"El-Kef?"

"The man who wants to see you."

The Frenchman waved his pistol and followed me into a softly-lit adjoining room where six small tables covered with white tablecloths stood. A scented candle burned in a red glass bowl in the center of each table. The far wall was covered with an assortment of old travel posters depicting scenes from places around the Mediterranean. Athens,

Tripoli, and Marrakech. Cairo, Beirut, and the island of Malta. One poster, larger than the others, showed a bearded Bedouin crouched down in the shade of a date palm tree, with a camel standing to one side. The shadows from the palm fronds spelled out *Tunisie* on the sand.

At the far end of the room was a service window. Through the window I saw a woman working in the kitchen beyond. She disappeared from my view before I could get a good look at her, but a moment later she stepped through the service door that led into the dining room. She looked startled when she saw myself and the Frenchman standing there.

I must have looked startled too. Because I had already seen her once that day. On the hillside road in front of the graveyard in Nice. And also the night before. When she pulled a gun on me in the café on the Rue de Catelet.

The dead woman wiped her hands on her apron.

The dead woman said, "Have you eaten?"

10

Her name wasn't Monika Robichaux. Her name was Aurora. At least, that's what she told me. At the moment I had no good reason to believe anything she said, and a fair number of good reasons not to.

She sat down and watched me in silence as I ate the bowl of fish soup that she'd brought. I was famished. I decided to concentrate on eating first and asking questions later. I washed the soup down with the white wine that she poured for me. The bottle sat on the table between us.

"I bear you no ill will," she said, when I had finished the soup and the glass of wine. Her eyes shifted away. "I was only doing what I was told. You'll need to talk to El-Kef."

I repeated the name. *El-Kef.* Wasn't that a city in Tunisia? I glanced up at the travel posters on the wall. "Did he take his name from one of these advertisements?"

"He took his name from his father, I imagine."

"So where is he?"

"His father?"

"Your boss."

"He's traveling back from Nice on his boat. He had to pull

into Cannes to make a repair. He'll be along in the morning."

"So I sit here and wait."

"We'll make you comfortable."

"The police think that you were murdered in an alley in Nice. I thought so too. Until I saw you in Nice. You were up on the hillside when the police showed up to arrest me this morning. Who tipped you off? The man from the consulate—Webb?"

A strained smile appeared on her face. "Actually, I heard about it on the police scanner. I only wanted to see for myself if they succeeded in capturing you. It might've changed things for me."

"Me too."

She said nothing.

"Two policemen are dead," I said. "Maybe the third one is dead too by now."

"I know nothing about that."

"And tell this El-Kef fellow that the police have the flash drive you left with me. They took it from me this morning in Nice, first thing. Tell him if he wants it back, he'll have to shake down the police."

The woman ignored that remark. She said, "Would you like more soup?"

She got up and reached across the table and picked up the empty soup bowl.

She disappeared into the kitchen.

The two men who had brought me inside had taken sandwiches from the kitchen. The Arab disappeared with his sandwich. The Frenchman sat down on a couch in the lobby to eat his. His pistol lay on the low table in front of the couch. He didn't look too worried about me. He could've picked up the pistol and aimed it and shot me and eaten another bite of his sandwich before I could make it out of my chair.

The woman returned with a full bowl of the soup and a smaller bowl filled with green olives and a tiny quiver of toothpicks. The thick soup was a disturbing shade of brown. I found two or three good-sized fish bones floating in it but I didn't carp. The woman refilled my wine glass and sat down again. I glanced at her now and then while I shoveled the soup down my throat.

She didn't say anything for a long time.

Then, "If it matters to you, Mister Slade, I was told only to give you the computer files. And take the money that you were supposed to give to me. I was also directed to keep a gun pointed at you to make sure that I got the money. That's all I know."

"You didn't get the money."

"You didn't give it to me."

"I didn't have it."

"I wasn't sure."

"I'm not the man you were looking for."

"I'm still not so sure."

"Does anyone know anything around here?"

The woman looked down and scratched her forearm absently. She'd taken her apron off. Her cotton chemise was striped in yellow and blue. When she looked at me again she said, "I can tell you this much. Sète is a place where a great deal of discretion is required. It was once a smuggling port. To some extent it still is. But the people here protect Ali El-Kef. He is one of the largest distributors of fresh fish in the south of France. He is very much an established business presence." She raised her hand to indicate the surroundings.

"He also owns this hotel."

I thought of Mahmoud's delivery truck, with the name of the fish supply firm—TRÉSOR DE LA MER S.A.—painted on the side. "So he told all of his drivers to keep an eye out for me. That's how I ran into Mahmoud."

"Mahmoud?"

I explained to her how I had come to meet the man named Mahmoud. "He even made me pay for the privilege of being hijacked. He took all the money in my wallet."

"He sounds like an audacious man."

"That would be one word for him."

"I don't think I know him." The woman speared an olive on the end of a toothpick and inspected it closely, as though it bore the characteristics of the man named Mahmoud. Then she dropped the olive into her mouth and chewed it slowly. After a moment she said, "There are many men who stay here. They come and go. Some of them drive the trucks. Some of them work on the boats or in the warehouses. It's been quite a long time since we've had a paying guest."

"I'm not a paying guest."

The woman dropped the toothpick in the bowl with the uneaten olives. "I wasn't referring to you."

"I'm a prisoner."

She frowned. "'Prisoner' is a little strong. As I understand it, you don't actually have any place else to go. What you need right now is rest. You can do that here."

"What I need right now is a battalion of lawyers."

The woman set her elbows on the table and rested her chin on her folded hands. Her face was a blank.

I said, "And what was all that business about a cigarette? In the café. You said you'd walk a mile for a Camel."

Slowly a smile took shape on her face. Followed by a soft laugh and a wry eyebrow. "It was a code phrase. You were supposed to respond. You were supposed to say, 'Time to light a Red and White.'"

"Quaint."

"Not so much."

I wondered if this woman knew Morgan. He was here in Sète, somewhere. Perhaps she'd heard of him. Sète wasn't a large town. If nothing else, she must've known where the restaurant called Le Poulet Ivre was. I wanted to ask her now. I wanted her to know that I wasn't here in Sète just because some fishmonger named El-Kef wanted me here. I had a friend here. A friend with clout. A friend who could pull strings. But as much as I wanted to say all of that, something told me not to. I decided to keep it under my hat, for the time being.

The woman picked up the empty soup bowl and the olive bowl and carried them into the kitchen. The meal was over. From the service window the woman called to the man on the couch in the lobby. His name was Benoit. He had been reading a newspaper and now he folded the newspaper and eased himself off the couch. He tucked the newspaper under his arm and picked up his pistol and motioned for me to follow him.

I walked out of the dining room.

"We have just the place for you," Benoit said. He pointed to the grand staircase.

Benoit followed me up the stairs.

I said, "What about the elevator?"

"Forget about the elevator."

On the fifth floor landing he directed me to walk down

a hallway lined with hotel room doors and peeling green wallpaper. At the end of the hallway he waved me aside and stepped up to a door, pulled a skeleton key from his pocket. Benoit worked the key up and down in the keyhole, then left and right. I noticed that there was also a dead bolt lock affixed to the door, and that the lock was operated from outside the room rather than from inside.

The room was small and spartan. Just a rutted spring bed and a wooden bureau that was missing a drawer. A bare light bulb burned in the ceiling fixture. Off to the left was a nook the size of a broom closet with a shower head and a porcelain sink and a toilet all built one on top of the other. A clean towel lay on the bed. A pitcher of water and a drinking glass rested on the bureau.

The one window in the room was covered on the outside by a metal screen that rolled up and down on wheels in a track. The type of screen used to protect windows during high winds and hard storms. The screen was locked to the sill with a padlock.

"Don't bother with the window," Benoit said. "There's nothing outside unless you feel like jumping five floors onto cobblestones. El-Kef will be back in the morning. He'll want to talk to you. Maybe he'll give you the grand tour of Sète. Or a ride in the U-boat."

"The U-boat?"

"His little toy." Benoit shrugged. He pulled the newspaper out from under his arm and tossed it onto the bed. "Take a look. You've made quite a splash."

Benoit departed, closing the door behind him. I heard metallic scraping as the skeleton key worked into the keyhole. It was followed by the click of the dead bolt sliding into place.

I went to the bed and picked up the newspaper. It was a copy of one of the Marseille newspapers, *Le Temps du Soleil*. The afternoon edition. My ability to read French isn't good but I didn't need to read French to examine the two photographs on the front page.

One of them was a photograph of the Nice street where the police and I had been ambushed that morning. The shot up remains of the police car could be seen behind a police barricade. The other picture was a poor reproduction of the photograph from my passport.

I read through the accompanying newspaper article as best I could.

According to the newspaper account, the national police blamed me for the murder of the woman in the alley, but that wasn't news. The woman was identified as Mlle. Monika Robichaux, 28, a French national recently employed in Great Britain. I thought of the photograph that Inspector Brissac had shown me at the police station. I didn't doubt that there was a dead woman and that the police had found her in an alley. But clearly the dead woman was not the woman I met in the café and I could prove it. All I had to do was drag the woman who called herself Aurora to the nearest police station.

But that wasn't a likely occurrence, any time soon.

The newspaper article had more about Robichaux. The National Police had identified her as a known associate of a group of eastern European criminals who called themselves the Rising Sun—an organization known to traffic in illicit drugs and weapons. It was believed that Robichaux was killed after she passed on sensitive information stolen from a British defense firm to a Rising Sun contact, a man who had arrived in Nice from Budapest.

An American named Richard Slade.

The ambush in Nice was explained as an attempt by the Rising Sun organization to rescue me from the police, or kill me to keep me from talking. They had accomplished neither objective, but two National Police officers were killed in the attempt. A third officer, *Gardien de la Paix Sébastien Lales*, was in critical condition in the intensive care unit at Saint Roch Hospital in Nice.

And I was still at large.

I continued reading. With a growing sense of disbelief. A police spokesperson stated that the sensitive information that Robichaux passed on was contained in files downloaded onto a common flash drive. The police had taken possession of the flash drive when I was detained in Nice. They had confirmed that the information on the flash drive was in fact the detailed plans for constructing a modern laboratory for the large-scale manufacture of *gaz moutarde*.

I puzzled over that for a moment.

Gaz moutarde.

Mustard gas.

Could that be right? I stared at the words. I knew vaguely what mustard gas was. I'd read about it in history books. It was a blister agent that had been used on the battlefield in World War I. First by the Germans, and then by the British, French, and Americans. According to the newspaper story, it was a particularly ghastly weapon because it was difficult to protect oneself against it. In severe cases, it caused a protracted and agonizing death. The story pointed out that it had been banned by the Geneva Protocols since 1925, but it was still used in certain remote corners of the globe. Usually by tyrants who couldn't afford the methods for mass killing that carried the Geneva Convention's seal of approval. The report noted that, most recently, mustard gas had been used by Saddam Hussein in northern Iraq, against the Kurdish population.

I stumbled through the article a second time, and then a third. Just to make sure I hadn't misunderstood what I was able to read. Then I set the newspaper aside and sat on the edge of the bed. Thinking hard.

I had never heard of a group of criminals called the Rising Sun. I knew nothing of a woman named Robichaux. And the references to mustard gas left me dumbstruck. Whatever was happening, it wasn't just a case of mistaken identity. I was being set up. By whom and for what reasons, I couldn't imagine. But right then, sitting alone in that room, I was convinced that the only way I'd be leaving France was in a box.

11

I woke up and felt a wave of panic wash over me. I couldn't recall where I was. The narrow bed and the cell-like room were entirely unfamiliar. Then slowly it came into focus. The hotel. The meal downstairs with the woman named Aurora. The imminent arrival of the man they called El-Kef. Slivers of muted light appeared around the edges of the metal screen that covered the window.

It was morning. Or perhaps afternoon.

I felt groggy. I had slept in my clothes and I had a crick in my neck from lying in an awkward position. I got up off the bed. I found a pair of clean dungarees, a black pullover sweater, and a pair of wool socks folded neatly on the bureau. To replace the dirty clothes that I had been wearing for the last two days. No shorts though. Maybe the hotel laundry was fresh out. The clothes hadn't been there the night before. Someone had been in the room while I slept. Had Aurora brought them in?

I took a quick shower and dressed. I noticed that my heavy coat was gone. Had I left it downstairs last night? I couldn't remember.

I was puzzling over the newspaper article again when I heard a key rattling in the door lock.

Then the dead bolt slid back.

Two men stood in the doorway. One of them walked straight to the tiny bathroom and looked around. His movements were quick and defensive, as though he expected trouble. The second one remained by the door.

The first one turned to me. He said, "Let's go."

I didn't bother to ask where.

We left the room and proceeded down the hallway. A man on either side of me, gripping my arms and rushing me along. One of the men was short, with a square head and a large chin that, judging from the scars on it, had come into contact with an immovable object once or twice. The other man was wide and round with a mouthful of small sharp teeth. The round one wore a black watch cap on his head and they both wore heavy dungarees, like the pair that I wore. Large steel-tipped work boots. Wool shirts over long-sleeved thermal undershirts. They looked like fishermen and they smelled of fish.

We raced down the five flights of stairs.

"Where's the fire?" I said.

Neither of them cared to tell me.

We crossed the deserted hotel lobby and pushed through the doorway that led into the white corridor I had come through from the garage the night before. We followed the corridor a short ways, turned into a dark connecting corridor on the right, stepped through another doorway, and descended into darkness on wooden steps that became rough stone halfway down. I smelled mold and mildew and sea water, and the odor of fish that permeated everything in Sète.

At the bottom of the stairs was a long tunnel with rough stone walls. I was following the round man now, with the square man behind me. We passed stone archways to the left and right. Beyond the archways were dark chambers that seemed to be storage areas for wooden crates and shipping containers of various sizes. In the dim light the chambers and the ancient stone walls looked medieval and sinister.

At the other end of the tunnel we climbed stone steps that led to an oaken door. We passed through the doorway and then climbed more steps. We were inside another building now. On the stairwell we passed a dirty window that looked out over a row of boats tied up to a pier, their bows bobbing in the roll of the tide. From what I could glimpse out the window, the pier was either connected to the building we were now in or the building itself was built on the pier.

At the top of the stairs the round man rapped on a wooden door. Then he turned the knob softly and I followed him inside, with a push from the square man behind me.

The room contained a non-descript wooden desk at one end and gray filing cabinets at the other. The floor was bare wood, gouged and stained with age. A table covered with nautical charts stood near the desk. Against the far wall was a black potbelly stove. The stove door was open and flames licked upward. A man knelt in front of the stove, stabbing at the flames with an iron poker. A stack of loose documents lay on the floor nearby and, after a moment, he reached over and grabbed a section of the stack and threw it into the stove. He pushed the papers around inside the stove with the poker, then added more documents to the flames. A length of stovepipe rose up into the ceiling but a fair amount of smoke was pouring out of cracks and holes in the pipe and collecting in the room. The gray light of day filtered in through a window near the stove.

The man at the stove stood up. He was middle-aged and of average height. His skin was light brown and his short hair was jet black with patches of gray above the ears. He wore a black eyepatch over one eye. His mouth looked like it had been sliced into his face with a sharp knife.

The man stepped forward. He held his arms out as though he intended to embrace me. His sweater and tan pants were smudged with ash.

"*Bonjour*, Mister Slade," he said.

The fact that the man still held the poker worried me. I took a step back but found that the square man was directly behind me. He pushed me forward. The man with the eyepatch dropped his arms to his sides and the tip of the poker hit the floor. He nodded at the round man and the round man departed quickly.

The square man remained behind me.

"I am Ali El-Kef," The man with the eyepatch said. "And you are now my guest."

"Why am I here?"

El-Kef turned his head so that his good eye peered at me sidewise. "We will address that delicacy in a moment."

El-Kef moved in close. He was still smiling when his knee came up and slammed into my crotch.

The pain shot upwards into my chest. My knees wobbled. I couldn't breathe. I doubled over. Tiny lights flashed at the edges of my vision. I heard the square man moving around behind me and wondered if there would be a blow coming from that direction. But no, he was merely preparing himself to grab me if I tried to fight back. I felt dizzy.

In short gasps my breath returned.

I waited for the pain and the dizziness to subside. After a minute I straightened up again. As best I could. I took several deep breaths. I tried to shake off the pain and the tiny flashing lights.

El-Kef studied me.

"I beg your forgiveness, Mister Slade," El-Kef said. "It was the will of Allah."

While I tried to compose myself, El-Kef stepped over to the desk. He bent down behind it and searched the desk drawers. He came up with a claw hammer in his hand.

The sight of the hammer gave me a start.

But it wasn't intended for me. A black laptop computer sat on the desk and now El-Kef went to work smashing it to pieces with the hammer. In a minute the computer was transformed into sharp pieces of plastic and micro-circuitry. El-Kef swept the pieces into an empty box and carried them to the window near the stove. He opened the window and glanced out. The he raised the box and poured the debris out the window.

"Only the sea keeps it secrets," he said.

He threw the box aside and closed the window and approached me again.

His one eye burned a hole through me.

He said, "Mister Slade, tell me about your work with the Rising Sun."

In these strained circumstances it took me a second to recall what or who the Rising Sun were—the terrorist organization that was named in the newspaper article I'd read.

"I don't know anything about them," I said. It was all I could say. It was the truth.

El-Kef pursed his lips and shook his head. I hadn't given him the answer that he wanted and now he looked disappointed. "You are here to destroy me," he said. "On whose behalf, I am not certain. But I do know that you will not succeed. I can disappear, in only a moment. A snap of my fingers. Nevertheless, I must know whom you are working for. Please grace me with an explanation."

I fixed my eyes on him. "Mister El-Kef, I don't know what you're talking about."

The insistent beep of a cell phone interrupted our debate. Maybe it was Allah, with further instructions. El-Kef fished the phone out of his pants pocket and raised it to his ear, said something in a language that I presumed was Bedouin. As El-Kef listened to the voice on the phone his face took on a distracted look and his gaze drifted upward to the ceiling. Then he lowered the phone and closed it with a hard and decisive snap and thrust it back into his pocket.

El-Kef said, "It has just been made known to me that I will be under attack soon. Right here in Sète. I am not certain, but I believe that it will be the Rising Sun who attacks me. So, I have no alternative but to prepare for a sea journey. Perhaps I'll return to my homeland of Algeria. I cannot say that the prospect of returning to couscous and bad plumbing excites me, but one must endure. What are your beliefs regarding Algeria, Mister Slade?"

I said nothing.

El-Kef placed his hands on his hips. Behind him the smoke continued to pour from the back of the stove and the seams of the stovepipe.

"The chances are good that you'll be traveling with me at least half the way across the sea," El-Kef said. "After that, it will be a matter of whether you can make yourself useful to me. If you do, then we will see Oran together. If not, then it will be interesting to learn how long serpents such as yourself can float."

El-Kef looked past me to the square man and gave him a nod. Suddenly the square man's muscled arms were looped under mine behind my back. The square man shifted his weight. Then he knocked my right leg out from under me and tossed me face down onto the floor.

12

The square man rested his knee in the small of my back while he tied my hands together behind me with a length of rope. When he was finished he let out a grunt that might have been satisfaction at a job well done, or it might have been just a grunt.

The rope was thick and rough. The square man bent down and pulled me up until I could get my feet under me.

El-Kef stood in front of me holding a battered pistol. The long barrel was pointed at my midriff.

El-Kef smiled. A strained smile that spread open like a crevice. "My choice of weaponry impresses you. It is German, of course—a Mauser. One of the first successful pistols of a semi-automatic type." El-Kef turned his hand and held the pistol closer. "Would you like to hear the noise it makes?"

"Not especially."

"I wonder if you would hear it. Or would the bullet travel through your gray matter to end your consciousness before the sound of the shot reached your ears. A question that you may soon resolve for yourself. If you cannot tell me what I want to know."

I was giving El-Kef the same answer as before when there was a knock at the door. A man in a green parka and a pair of black Wellington waterproof boots stepped into the room.

My head was still turned to observe the new arrival when El-Kef smashed the pistol into the side of my face. My vision blurred but, oddly, I felt no pain. Maybe I was getting used to being knocked around. The square man held on to me to keep me from falling sideways to the floor. I kept my eyes closed and shook my head. Trying to clear my vision of the tiny flickering lights that had returned.

I heard El-Kef ask the new man a question in French. Something to do with a tunnel and whether or not it was in order. I didn't quite follow it but I assumed they were talking about the tunnel that led from the hotel. The man said that he'd finished the job and El-Kef ordered him to proceed downstairs.

The man in the Wellingtons departed.

Somehow I got my eyes back on track.

El-Kef turned back to me. "Let us get on with this, Mister Slade. Time is now lacking. What is your purpose here?"

I told him what I could tell him. I told him the truth. I had come to the French Riviera to visit a friend who was staying in Antibes. In Nice I ran into the woman who worked in El-Kef's hotel. She slipped a computer flash drive into my coat pocket. Later I was picked up by the French police and, later still, my police escort and myself were ambushed on our way to the National Police headquarters in Nice. Since that time I had been on the run. Hoping that I could find the friend I'd come to see. He was here in the south of France, somewhere. I hoped that he could help me.

El-Kef's forehead furrowed. "His name is what?"

I took a chance and told him. "His name is Septimus Morgan."

El-Kef shook his head. "His name is Ivashko."

I tried to protest, to correct him once again, but El-Kef raised his hand for silence. "Shut up and listen to me, I am speaking to you. The *Police Nationale* are using the incident in Nice that you were so deeply involved in as an excuse to hunt down the people of the Rising Sun, all across France. For a reason that is unknown to me the police believe that I am one of these people. But I am most certainly not. Equally inexplicable to my feeble mind is the fact that the Rising Sun has also decided that I must die. Perhaps you can help me to understand these things. I have already posed these questions to your estimable colleague—Ivashko. He has not been so helpful."

My estimable colleague? My confusion grew deeper. Seemed to fall into a dark pit and keep falling. El-Kef stared at me. His eye looked deep, soulless, and empty. I noticed that the side of my face where El-Kef had hit me with the flat side of the Mauser had gone numb. I pushed my tongue around inside my mouth. All my teeth seemed to be present.

Now El-Kef nodded to himself.

"Very well then," he said. "Let us go talk to your friend. Perhaps he can help you to remember these things. I'm keeping him in the U-boat. Which is where you may find yourself also, after all has become known under the eye of Allah."

El-Kef motioned with the pistol.

The square man hustled me out of the office and into the hallway. With El-Kef right behind us, humming a delicate tune to himself. *Under the eye of Allah*. I wondered if, having only one working orb himself, El-Kef had invested his God with the same defect.

I was led farther into the building. We reached a stairway and descended. Suddenly I realized where I was. Directly across the short hallway was the staircase that the round and square men had led me up earlier, on our way to El-Kef's office. To my left was the thick oak door that lead into the tunnel and back to the hotel. The building was laid out like a rat maze.

But we didn't return to the tunnel.

Instead, we passed through a pair of swinging stainless steel doors and stepped out onto a large platform that formed the end of a boat dock—a large U-shaped indoor dock protected by the shell of a building the size of a warehouse. The piers on each side of the central platform extended to the far end of the cavernous building where a sectioned aluminum door was raised to allow access to the harbor waters. The dock and the tall canopy over it were the seaward side of the same building we had just come from.

The platform we stood on and the two piers attached to it were covered with worn-down maritime machinery, piles of yellow fishing nets and red buoys, and stacks of wooden shipping crates that looked much the same as the crates I'd seen in the tunnel.

Tied to mooring posts along the pier to the left was a fishing boat.

The boat was perhaps seventy feet long and twenty feet wide. White with faded red trim. There was a wide pilothouse and radio antennas affixed to a central mast and cargo hatches fore and aft. The bow of the boat pointed out at the harbor. The stern of the boat was a dozen feet or so from the edge of the platform we stood on.

The name painted in black lettering on the stern was *Le Branledore*.

A gangplank led from the pier onto the boat's fore deck. At the moment two men dressed in work clothes were busy loading the boat's forward cargo hold with crates taken from stacks on the pier. One of the men was the man I had seen earlier in the office, the one wearing the black Wellington boots. The crates were relatively small, but from the way the men labored, they must've been heavy. I could see serial numbers and other nomenclature stenciled on the crates. They looked like the kinds of crates one might pack weapons in. Or ammunition. Or high explosives.

They didn't look like boxes of fishing gear.

I was led along the pier to the gangplank. The two men paused in their work as the square man pushed me across the gangplank and onto the boat. El-Kef followed. The deck was slippery and I nearly lost my footing as I was guided to the stern of the boat.

Attached to the aft deck was a hoist rig. A steel cable hung from the end of the boom down into the water. The other end of the cable was attached to an electric winch behind the pilothouse. A burly man in waterproof work pants stood at the winch, idly drinking from a thermos. El-Kef motioned to him and the man set his thermos aside and reached down. In a second the electric motor that operated the winch began to whine. The whining grew as the winch kicked in against the tension on the cable.

I was pushed up to the gunwale at the stern of the boat. I looked down and saw that the patch of harbor water between the stern and the central platform of the dock was roiling. Something connected to the other end of the cable was rising out of the water.

It was a cage.

A rusted steel cage.

The cage was not much more than four feet from top to bottom, with each of the four sides probably three feet in width. A large hook at the end of the cable was attached to a round metal eye that protruded from the top of the cage. The bars of the cage were spaced four or five inches apart.

When the cage was fully out of the water the whine of the winch motor changed as the man operating the apparatus disengaged the motor. The cage stopped rising. It hung in the air a few feet from the stern of the boat, dripping sea water and swinging slightly at the end of the steel cable.

Folded up inside the cage was a man.

He was positioned on his buttocks with his legs folded up in front of him. His knees rested under his chin. His arms were pushed tight against his sides and his hands gripped the steel bars in front of him. Except for a pair of boxer shorts he was naked. His skin was pale white and his head hung loosely to one side. His eyes were closed.

Pieces of seaweed and other small bits of flotsam clung to his bare skin. He looked like he'd been dragged along the bottom of the sea.

I was sure he was dead.

And that I was next.

El-Kef gave the corpse inside the steel cage an appraising look. A little skeptical. Like El-Kef had set out a trap and this was what he'd caught and he wasn't sure what to do with it, what it was good for.

The corpse moved.

A slight movement. A shifting of the torso.

Followed by a faint moan.

I was stunned. I thought I was watching someone come back from the dead. The man's head rose an inch or two. The eyes opened. They looked red and cloudy and distant. The mouth fell open. The man coughed and spit and shook his head. I could see now the bruises and red gashes on his face and more dark bruises across his arms and legs.

He'd been beaten quite thoroughly before he was fitted into the cage.

When the man let go of the steel bars and let his hands slide down to his shins I saw something else too. On his left forearm was a large tattoo. A long ovoid shape with a smaller ovoid attached to one end of it. Small dark lines, bent sharply in places, radiated out from the larger egg shape. It looked like a silhouette of some type of insect. A beetle or a cockroach.

El-Kef motioned toward the cage. "How do you like my device, Mister Slade? I pack difficult men into it and lower them into the sea until they struggle to keep their noses above the water. Then I leave them there. Sometimes for many hours. Sometimes for a day. The motionings of the tide are treacherous when the difference between breathing and certain death is a few millimeters. But when these men emerge from the sea they are less difficult. If they are still alive."

I stared at the man in the cage. Watched as he tried slowly and painfully to shift his position a few inches. As best as I could tell he was middle-aged, perhaps forty years old. Dark hair cut close to the scalp. Dark bloodshot eyes that seemed to swim in his eye sockets.

The man let out a long liquid cough and spit out phlegm.

Then pulled his lips back against his teeth. It looked like the snarl of a feral animal.

"Last night this boat was docked in Cannes," El-Kef said to me. He spoke now with a studied casualness, as though trying to impart to me an extra measure of horror by seeming to take this vision of hell in stride, just business as usual. "My men and I were elsewhere on a matter of business and we discovered this man searching the cabin below when we returned. He has said very little so far, but there is one thing that I already know to be true. He is linked to the Rising Sun. Just as I believe you are."

"I've never seen this man."

"His name is Igor Ivashko. But perhaps it is also Morgan."

"I don't care what he calls himself. I don't know him."

"We shall see."

El-Kef turned back to the man in the cage. The man's eyes wandered as El-Kef raised the Mauser pistol—I'd almost forgotten that he had the weapon in his hand. El-Kef extended his arm and pointed the pistol at the man in the cage and aimed down the barrel. El-Kef shouted the man's name. Then, in French, he told the man that he had one last chance to save himself.

The caged man didn't respond.

He didn't seem to understand.

El-Kef turned to the square man and said something in Bedouin.

The square man stepped out from behind me and approached the gunwale. He began shouting at the man now too, in a Slavic tongue.

The man in the cage came to life. He began to respond in what sounded like the same Slavic language that the square man had used. As he talked his voice became stronger and his tone more hostile. The tendons in his neck stood out in sharp relief and he began to shout. El-Kef stared at the man with contempt. He kept the barrel of the Mauser pointed at the cage.

Then Ivashko stopped shouting. As suddenly as he'd started. He fell silent and closed his eyes.

El-Kef looked to the square man for a translation. Speaking in Bedouin the square man explained to his boss the nature of the tirade the man named Ivashko had just unleashed. El-Kef nodded and shrugged his shoulders, not too bothered. I glanced at the man standing beside the winch. He looked bored. The two men on the other side of the boat were still at work loading the wooden crates into the forward cargo hold.

El-Kef lowered the pistol and tucked the barrel awkwardly into the waist of his pants. The wooden pistol butt protruded out from under his sweater like an abnormal growth. El-Kef motioned to the winch man and the winch man reached down, picked up a wooden pole that was six or seven feet in length. He brought it over and handed it to his boss, then returned to his position beside the winch.

El-Kef hefted the pole and took hold of it at one end with both hands. He stepped close to the gunwale and took careful aim and then thrust the tip of the pole between the bars of the cage.

The man inside erupted in screams of pain.

El-Kef rammed the pole into the cage again and again. Hitting the man in the legs, the stomach, the chest and neck, the head. The man continued to scream as he tried to protect himself. Tried to cover his stomach with his bent legs. Tried to protect his face with his hands. But it was no use. He didn't have enough freedom of movement inside the cage.

He could only scream.

It was quite a commotion. Difficult to ignore. And I wasn't ungrateful for the distraction that occupied El-Kef and his men. I didn't need them watching me as I worked a little more slack in the knot that tied my hands together.

But even if I could free my hands, then what? El-Kef still had his pistol. Maybe the square man and even the man operating the winch had weapons of their own. I waited. Unsure of what to do. But certain that I wouldn't let them stuff me into the cage. Into the U-boat.

The cries of the broken figure inside the cage subsided into a wail. After several more jabs with the pole El-Kef paused for breath. Torture was hard work, he needed a rest.

"Ivashko, your situation is quite hopeless," El-Kef said, once again speaking in French, even though the man didn't seem familiar with the language. "You will talk to me now or you will die."

El-Kef turned and shouted to the man beside the winch. The man engaged the winch motor and the cage began to descend. The caged man screamed as the bottom edges of the cage hit the cold murky water. His feet disappeared under the water, then his ankles and shins and waist and elbows. He raised his chin as the water reached his neck and let out one last gut-wrenching cry.

El-Kef was motioning to the winch man to stop the descent of the cage into the water when a faint beeping sound began. El-Kef set the pole down and pulled his cell phone out of his pants pocket and opened it up. He spoke into it in his native tongue and then he listened. A deep frown appeared on his face. I saw that the square man kept his attention on the man in the cage while El-Kef was distracted by the phone call, and so I continued to work more slack into the knot in the rope that bound my hands. I thought now that with one or two hard pulls I could squeeze one hand free. I glanced at the man by the winch and turned a little to keep my hands out of his line of sight. I kept on maneuvering my left hand and pulling at the knot.

El-Kef glanced at his watch now. He said something further into the phone and listened some more and then closed the phone. He looked dismayed. Bad news had arrived. El-Kef turned to the square man and said something in Bedouin. The square man immediately left the stern of the boat and walked quickly into the pilot house.

Then El-Kef turned and shouted in French to the two men who were loading the last few boxes from the pier onto the boat. I didn't catch most of what he said to them, but from the tone of his voice and the way the men suddenly began working at double speed it was clear that it was time to leave.

Just then I heard the rumble of the diesel engines below deck. For a second the patch of deck under my feet shook and shivered. Then the engines settled into a throaty idle. The square man in the pilot house was preparing the boat for departure.

Just El-Kef and the winch man on the aft deck now—no one else.

It was now or never.

13

I was thankful for the noise of the boat engines.

It helped to cover the sounds I made as I struggled with the rope.

I extended the fingers of my left hand and pressed them together as tightly as I could. I tucked my thumb along the underside of the fingers. Then I pulled hard on the rope. It was caught around my knuckles. I felt the warmth of my own blood on my fingers. I glanced around. The man beside the winch was fiddling with the machinery. El-Kef was now pulling the pistol from the waistband of his pants. He looked like he had reached a decision about Ivashko.

I pulled at the rope and kept pulling. I had almost given up when suddenly I felt the rope slide roughly over the abraded knuckles of my left hand.

I had done it. My hands were free. But El-Kef had finally noticed my movements out of the corner of his eye. He turned toward me sharply, swinging the pistol around.

The next moment was a blur. I acted on pure fear. I jumped forward and brought my fist up and threw the hardest punch that I could muster. A roundhouse of considerable proportions. Directly into El-Kef's face.

The momentum of the blow carried me forward. I nearly lost my balance. I saw El-Kef land hard on his back on the deck. He lost his grip on the pistol and it slid away from him. I raced after it and picked it up and leveled it at the winch man, who had seen what had just happened to his boss and was taking tentative steps toward me.

The pistol gave him the reason he needed to stay out of the fight. He raised his hands and stepped back.

El-Kef rolled onto his side. He started to get up, then saw me standing nearby with the pistol in my hand.

El-Kef began shouting at the top of his lungs.

The two men who had been loading the boat were both on the pier now. They heard El-Kef's cries for help and saw me with the antique Mauser in my hand. One of the men—Wellington—reached behind his back and removed an automatic pistol from under his wool sweater. The other man just clenched his fists as he ducked down and moved toward the gangplank.

For a half second I felt certain that my escape had ended before it began. I couldn't run toward the gangplank. And I couldn't go over the starboard side of the boat—there was a good thirty feet of water between the boat and the far pier. Wellington would pick me off before I'd swum half the way. And there was at least a dozen feet of water between the stern of the boat and the platform at the rear of the dock. It was too far to jump.

But there was the cage.

The top of the cage was still a few inches above the water. The man inside clung to the horizontal bars just above his head. All that was visible were the clenched hands and the man's forehead and nose and two round red eyes filled with stark terror.

There was nothing I could do to help him. But there was something he could do for me.

I took a running jump up onto the gunwale and kept going. As I cannoned off the stern of the boat I pushed off hard with my right leg. My left foot landed on the top of the steel cage. I felt the cage start to shift in the water under my weight and momentum. But I was already jumping off the cage, using the momentum of the original jump to propel myself forward.

A gunshot rang out. My right foot landed on the edge of the dock. Then my left foot.

But I was off balance.

I hunched my back and bent forward, stretching my arms out as far as I could in a desperate attempt to regain my balance. For one long frozen moment my body seemed to be caught at exactly the point where the prospects of falling forward onto the dock or backward into the water were entirely equal.

Then time began moving again. I fell forward and landed on my hands and knees on the dock.

A second shot rang out. Wellington was moving among the crates and machinery on the pier. I scrambled to my feet and ran. Hell-bent. Wellington crouched down behind a pile of buoys and got another shot off. I heard a sharp noise and saw a patch of the coated surface of the dock erupt into a plume of wood splinters.

Wellington was getting his range.

I ducked behind a large shipping crate just as the sound of the next shot reached my ears. I crouched down and tried to catch my breath. I was safe, for the moment. But it was a precarious moment. I checked the Mauser pistol over as best I could. I found the magazine release and checked the clip. It was full, as near as I could tell.

I slipped the clip back in and peered around the edge of the crate.

I expected to see Wellington and the other man moving along the pier toward me. Maybe even the square man from the boat's pilothouse, and El-Kef too. All of them armed and running forward from one defensive position to the next, cool and professional, until they boxed me in and captured me, or killed me.

But that wasn't what I saw.

What I saw was the boat's stern hunker down in the water while the bow raised up. What I heard was the sudden gurgling roar of the boat's engines at full throttle. Strangely, the gangplank hadn't been pulled in, and as the boat plowed forward the unarmed man from the dock ran across it. The man jumped and landed in a heap on the boat deck just as the gangplank fell away from the pier and landed in the water.

Rather than trying to pull it aboard, the man pushed the other end over the side of the boat.

I saw El-Kef on the aft deck, crouched down behind the gunwale and looking in my direction. The winch man was frantically pulling a mooring rope onto the deck and the square man was nowhere in sight. The bow of the boat rose higher as the propellers thrashed the water and the diesel engines roared. I realized that the steel cage with the man inside was dragging behind the boat—I could just make out the top of the cage in the roiling water of the boat's wake.

El-Kef turned and motioned to the winch man. The winch

man dropped the mooring rope and ran unsteadily to the winch. He grasped the control lever. A second later the top of the cage disappeared under the froth of water. Then, as the boat reached the entrance to the covered dock and pushed out under the gray sky into the harbor, the winch end of the cable spun off the end of the boom. The cable whipped around in the air, then fell into the water and disappeared as it followed the cage down into the depths.

The U-boat had submerged for the last time. The man in the rusty cage was sleeping with the fish now.

El-Kef's boat plowed across the harbor at top speed. The sound of the straining diesel engines grew distant. I raised my head above the edge of the shipping crate, looking for the swinging metal doors that I had come through on the way in. The doors were nearby, I was sure.

Then another gunshot rang out. The round tore into the edge of the shipping crate, a few inches from my shoulder.

I ducked back down.

Wellington was still here. Hidden among the crates and buoys and machinery. I started moving in a crouch to my left. I reached a wide space between two crates. As I ran out into the open I fired a round wildly at the spot where I had last seen Wellington. The Mauser kicked and almost jumped out of my hand when I pulled the trigger.

Then I spotted the doors.

I was closer than I thought.

I fired again as I ran in a high-speed crouch the last few yards to the swinging doors. Another gunshot from Wellington echoed through the building. I could only hope that Wellington was as bad a shot as I was.

The doors were right in front of me. I dived and slid feet

first into them and scrambled the rest of the way through.

The doors swung shut behind me.

I jumped up with the pistol raised. I felt the adrenaline coursing through my body. The hallway was empty. There was only the oak door with the iron fittings, about fifty feet ahead. And, to either side, the stairs that led to the upper floors of the building that adjoined the covered dock. The concrete floor was wet. Water had puddled in the low spots. As I ran I could feel the blood pulsing in my ringing ears.

The door leading into the tunnel was thirty feet away. Now twenty feet. I expected to hear the doors behind me swing open any second now. Then the hallway would fill with the sound of one last gunshot and I would be sent sliding face-first through puddles of fish-smelling water. With a small bullet hole in my back and a much larger and uglier hole in my chest.

Another thought flashed in my mind, clear and bright. I didn't want to die. I had not lived all of my life, trying my best to do what is good and proper, only to end it in a bare fish-smelling water-puddled hallway leading to a dark tunnel in a shady port town on the wrong side of the south of France. I can't account for that thought, or why it occurred to me in just that way, but it is still vivid in my mind.

But, thankfully, there was no gunshot.

The doors behind me remained closed.

I reached the heavy oak door and pulled it open. The bottom of the door scraped along the concrete floor. I scrambled through the doorway and jumped down the stone steps and ran on across the rough stones of the tunnel floor. The overhead lights in their glass casings were still on.

As I passed the first storage room off the main tunnel I

noticed two wires, one blue and one white, that appeared out of the darkness and ran along the floor of the tunnel toward the next storage room. I didn't recall seeing them on my first journey through the tunnel and I wondered why they were there. They looked clean and new. I remembered something that El-Kef had said up in the office. El-Kef had asked Wellington if the tunnel work was done. As I ran on, I wondered what sort of tunnel work had needed to be done. And whether it involved blue and white wires.

A second later I found out.

The explosion lifted me into the air and sent me tumbling forward. The concussion from the blast felt like someone with large hands had slapped them hard over my ears. Small pieces of stone hit me from every direction. I landed on the rough stone floor and rolled and finally came to rest, flat on my back. The passageway had disappeared into a great cloud of dust.

The lights flickered, then went out.

I sat up and tried to shake off the effects of the blast. My hearing seemed to have abandoned me for the moment. I noticed that, through some small miracle or accident of fate, I still held the pistol in my hand. I was gripping the butt so hard that my hand shook.

I got to my feet and I tucked the pistol into the back of my pants. I could see nothing. I moved forward. I walked unsteadily for a few feet, waving my arms before me in the darkness. My right hand came into contact with the stone wall. That was good. If the wall was here then the stairs had to be in this other direction. Unless I was heading the wrong way, back toward the dock. Hard to tell. I took a chance and pressed on, reaching out for a patch of wall here and there to guide me in the darkness. Except for the breaks in the wall for the entrances to the storage rooms, the system worked rather well.

Until the second explosion hit me like a hammer.

My legs flew out from under me. I landed hard, all in a heap, like a load of logs falling off a truck. A large piece of stone hit me in the back of head. I gasped and coughed and struggled to breathe. The air was thick. It tasted like chalk and coated the back of my throat. I struggled to get to my feet. I took a few hesitant steps forward.

Then, unaccountably, one of the overhead lights at the far end of the tunnel flickered back on.

That was a bit of luck. The first explosion had knocked out the lights and now the second explosion had jarred the connections enough to bring one of them back on. But I couldn't count on the light burning for long. My hearing returned just in time to catch the sounds of timbers cracking and stones falling and the rush of soil pouring down. A stretch of tunnel behind me was collapsing in on itself.

I ran toward the light. Just as I had done in the passageway after the ambush in Nice. Running for my life toward a distant patch of light seemed to be the sum total of my recent experience. I hoped that I was getting good at it. I saw the stairs ahead. Only a short way to go. I ran harder. Breathing in the chalky dust. I heard more rumbling behind me. What was above the tunnel? A building? A street? Whatever was up there, it was going to disappear into a large dusty hole.

I was twenty-five feet from the stairs when the one light flickered out again. I ran on in the darkness, picking my feet up high to keep myself from tripping on the rough stones and debris. When I thought I was near the stairs I slowed down and walked forward carefully. Kicking my feet out to feel for the first stair step.

I found it.

I raced up the stairs, one hand sliding along the wall to guide me. At the top of the stairs I pushed open the door. I stumbled out of the dark side-hallway and into the main hallway and collapsed on the floor. I gulped air while my eyes adjusted to the bright light from the fluorescent tubes overhead. My legs were weak and shaking. I realized how close I had been to death.

But there was no time to rest. I heard shouts coming from the direction of the garage. I pulled myself together and got to my feet. I headed in the other direction, toward the white door that led into the hotel lobby. My nerves were stretched razor-sharp. My head buzzed with fear and adrenaline.

I dashed out into the lobby and waved the Mauser pistol around, but the lobby was empty. The dining room looked empty as well. Ahead of me were the pebbled-glass front doors. Still closed and, presumably, still locked. It occurred to me that I could shoot the glass out of the front doors and escape into the street. But it might be best to slip away more quietly, if that was possible. Maybe I could escape out the back, through the kitchen—there must be a door back there. Perhaps a door that opened into an alley.

I had just turned toward the dining room when a figure emerged from the shadows up on the landing of the grand staircase to my left.

The figure spoke.

"Drop the gun."

I looked up. Shocked to see that I was not alone.

It was the woman. Aurora. She looked much the same as

she had the night before. Except that she had no apron on. And instead of a thin cotton chemise she now wore a heavy black turtleneck sweater. Black turtleneck sweaters seemed to be the garment of choice in this town. But I wasn't so concerned about her sartorial views. What captured my attention was the large revolver in her hand. And the fact that it was pointed at me.

I let the Mauser fall from my hand.

Then she fired.

14

I was looking directly at Aurora when she fired. I knew, without a doubt, that I was a dead man. The bullet would tear through my chest and the blackness would descend and that would be all. The fact that at least I wouldn't die in the fish-smelling hallway that I'd left behind downstairs was small comfort.

But I was still standing when the reverberations from the gunshot died out in my ears.

I heard a noise behind me and I turned, my hands half raised. In the dining room doorway a man in dungarees writhed on the floor. His blood-covered hands clutched his blood-covered neck. His eyes looked too round and too wide. His mouth was open and choking sounds came out and his fat pink tongue seemed to want to escape down the side of his whiskered face. The man twisted one way and then another. He looked like a snake trying to cough up a particularly large rodent that had refused to be swallowed.

Then the writhing stopped. There was a long raspy noise and then that stopped too.

The man lay still. His too-round eyes stared at nothing.

The machine gun that he'd carried with him lay on the linoleum floor.

I turned back to Aurora.

She stood now at the bottom of the staircase. I saw the fear in her eyes but there was a hardness there too. She pointedly avoided looking at the man she'd just shot and killed. She studied my face instead. After a moment she stepped over and looked down at the Mauser and kicked it aside.

The silence was broken by a sudden commotion upstairs, sounded like a door being kicked in.

Aurora said, "I just saved your life, Mister Slade. With that in mind, how far can I trust you?"

Her voice sounded distant. For a second I thought it was a rhetorical question. It wasn't. I said the only thing I could think of to say. "How far do you need to trust me?"

"Some men have broken into one of El-Kef's warehouses," she said. "On the other side of the port. I don't know who they are, but there was shooting. I'm afraid that they will be here in the hotel at any moment. We can escape but we must go now."

Aurora stepped around me. She kept her head turned away from the corpse as she bent down and picked up the dead man's machine gun. She paused, studying the weapons in her hands. She seemed to be having second thoughts.

Aurora raised the revolver, held it flatwise. "Do you know how to use this?"

"Aim. Pull the trigger. Hope for the best."

"That's not reassuring."

She handed me the pistol. I gripped the butt and kept the barrel pointed at the floor.

Aurora walked into the dining room, pulled a white

tablecloth from one of the tables. She wrapped the machine gun up in the cloth until the outline of the weapon was well obscured.

She tucked the wrapped gun under her arm.

I said, "Why are you helping me?"

She didn't answer. She stepped past me on her way to the front doors, motioning for me to follow her.

The doors were unlocked now. They opened easily. She peered out.

"The street looks empty," she said. "Keep the pistol under your sweater. If you notice anyone in the street looking too concerned about us then walk faster. If you see guns in their hands then go ahead and shoot. Does all of this sound agreeable?"

She explained that she had a car parked in one of the city parking lots. The lot was situated next to one of the stone bridges along the canal. It would be a walk of perhaps five hundred feet. But there was no way of knowing who we might encounter. The men who had attacked El-Kef's warehouse seemed to be converging *en masse* on the town.

"Is it the Rising Sun?" I said.

"I don't know. One of the men from the docks called up here. He said they were under attack. By men in civilian clothes who were well-kitted out with weapons. I think we can safely say that they are not the police. Or fish merchants."

Aurora turned and stepped outside. I tucked the pistol into my pants and pulled my sweater over it and followed her out. There seemed to be no other option. I had to trust this woman. With a bit of luck maybe she could get me out of this wretched town. Then we'd see what was what.

Daylight was fading. The chill of the sea air felt bracing

against my face. We crossed the street, walking quickly, fighting the urge to run. There was a single car coming down the street from the left, followed closely by a large black van. The car was small—an Opel sedan with a crooked front bumper. Probably not the sort of vehicle that one uses when unfolding a plan to take over a hotel by force.

But the black van gave me pause.

We reached the far side of the street and within a few seconds we had rounded the corner. The façade of the hotel was now out of sight behind us. I mentioned the black van. Aurora merely nodded. I kept my hand over the pistol that was hidden under my sweater to keep it from falling out of my pants.

Aurora walked with long purposeful strides. The machine gun stayed wrapped up and tucked under her arm. Her eyes were watchful and her jaw set. I supposed that carrying a high-powered machine gun with the intention of using it at the drop of the first hat gives one a hard cast of mind. I wondered where she fit into all of this. Was I making a mistake by coming with her?

We crossed two more streets before we made it to the canal along the Quai de Leopold Suquet. Small boats moored along the sea walls bobbed softly in the water. The street on the far side of the canal was lined with dusty shops and seafood restaurants, with two or three ancient hotels rising a few floors above the ragged hodgepodge of rooftops. The cries of seagulls filled the air.

As we crossed the stone bridge I heard the buzz of a helicopter in the distance.

We reached the car park and I followed Aurora to a brown Renault sedan. She unlocked the car and we climbed in and she handed me the machine gun wrapped in the table cloth. I pulled out the pistol and set it on the floor and set the machine gun on my lap. Aurora started the car. The dashboard rattled as the engine sputtered to life.

I said, "Where are we going?"

"Marseille."

"Any particular reason?"

"I know people there who can help us."

"I need to get out of the country."

"They can arrange that."

"How much will it cost?"

Aurora said nothing. She wrestled the manual transmission into reverse. With a sharp jolt we backed out of the parking stall. She shifted into first gear. The engine shook and shuddered as we drove out of the car park and onto the street. As a getaway car the Renault left something to be desired.

"You'll have to tell them everything you know," Aurora said now. "About what happened in Nice."

"Who are these people?"

"It doesn't matter."

"It does to me."

Aurora didn't answer.

We followed the twisting streets up the hill behind the old port. Soon we were out of town and driving along a winding country road in the gloaming. The surface of the road was uneven and the car rocked from side to side on bad springs. I thought about what I had read in the newspaper about the Rising Sun and I wondered what Aurora's interest in this situation was. It was clear to me now that she was more than a woman who helped run El-Kef's hotel.

"What's your connection to the Rising Sun?" I said.

"I don't work for them, if that's what you mean."

"But El-Kef does. Or he did. Am I right?"

"That's a question for El-Kef."

"Was it the Rising Sun who wanted you to impersonate the Frenchwoman in Nice?"

Aurora slammed her foot on the brake. The tires screeched against the pavement and I was thrown forward in the seat. The car shuddered to a halt in the middle of the road. She looked at me with anger. Her hands were locked tight on the steering wheel, ten and two.

"Get out," she said.

"So you can shoot me?"

"So you can leave. I have business to attend to. If you're going to insist on being a dead weight, then sink on your own."

"You can't blame me for wondering who you are."

"What will it be, Mister Slade?"

There was a long awkward silence.

I stayed in the car.

We drove on for several miles in a further silence. Night descended and the road grew crooked. When Aurora spoke again her tone had changed. Her anger had passed. It had probably been nothing more than her frayed nerves catching up with her. She even sounded a little apologetic now, although I may have imagined that.

"Tell me about Nice," she said. She kept her eyes on the road ahead. "What happened?"

"If you watch the television, you already know."

"I want to hear it from you."

"It sounds better on television."

We passed a road sign that said we had 110 kilometers to

travel before we reached Marseille. I sat back with my arms folded and tried to recall what I could of the events in Nice. It was hard to believe that it had all transpired only two days before. That I had come to France to meet an old friend. With a manuscript of poems on a flash drive. That I had taken a room at the Negresco and had gone out to dinner. So far so good. But then I had met Aurora at the café and she had pulled a gun on me and things began to spin out of control. First in a long wide spiral and then tighter and tighter. Like being sucked down a drain.

Then there was Brissac from the National Police. And the ambush. There was the American consular deputy who had turned me in to the police and then Mahmoud and his fish truck and El-Kef and his oblique concerns. And the dead man imprisoned in the U-boat cage. I had thought it might be good to unburden myself of this crazed tale, but it wasn't. It all seemed too bizarre to credit. The only fitting end to the tale would be if I suddenly woke up in a psychiatric ward, shackled to a bed. That would have been the best of all possible worlds. To know that I had gone mad and the rest of the world was still reliably sane.

But I knew that was not the case. There was nothing wrong with my mind.

It was the world that had gone mad.

Aurora said nothing as I spoke. The engine of the Renault battered on underneath the hood. We sped into a long curve and Aurora concentrated on keeping the Renault on the road. Did Aurora believe me? I hoped that she did. I needed someone to believe me. I needed someone in my corner. Or I would surely be lost.

15

We drove on. The night seemed darker now. When Aurora spoke there was resolve in her voice. Something had been decided.

"Where were you at, before you arrived in Nice?" she said.

"Budapest."

"What were you doing there?"

"Negotiating a business deal."

"Pesticides, I think you said."

"I told you all of this."

"Tell me again."

"I've said my piece. Tell me yours."

Aurora kept her eyes on the road. Her face was an expressionless mask. I wondered again who she truly was. She sighed. "All right," she said. "This is what I know. The Rising Sun organization originated in Georgia—the former Soviet republic. At the start they were nothing more than a loose gang of petty criminals and adventurers. Then a man named Nikolai Kalugin took control. He had slightly higher aspirations than the others. He knew of a supply of weapons-grade uranium that was stored at a nuclear facility in a remote part of Georgia. The facility was no longer in service and the security at the site was poor.

"Kalugin engineered the theft of the uranium. Eventually he sold it to one of the more powerful African markets who, no doubt, had other buyers lined up. The profits were large—so large that Kalugin saw where the future of the Rising Sun lay. The former Soviet Union was full of all manner of military weapons and equipment that were left to rust when the government collapsed and the Soviet Army was hung out to dry. The Rising Sun began stealing entire arsenals from military depots and selling them on the black market.

"The organization grew as the money rolled in. They extended their operations into new areas. Romania, Hungary, Bulgaria. Any place where military weapons could be stolen easily and resold for a significant profit. Inevitably, they also began trafficking in illegal drugs on a rather large scale. Right now the Rising Sun conducts its business all over Europe, including here in France."

"Where does El-Kef fit in?"

A grim smile crossed Aurora's face. "I don't know if El-Kef was one of them or not. But I'm sure he's not one now. He has had his own smuggling operation for many years. I suppose it wouldn't be odd if he had run across the Rising Sun once or twice, or that they ran across him."

"The man that El-Kef was holding prisoner at the boat dock—the one in the cage. El-Kef thought he was working for the Rising Sun too."

"Is that right?" Aurora sounded surprised.

"His name was Igor Ivashko."

"How would you know that?"

"El-Kef mentioned his name."

Aurora looked taken aback by the news. Her hand came up to her face as though she could see clearly the horror of Ivashko's death and it shocked her. Then I realized that she wasn't thinking about Ivashko at all. She was looking hard into the rearview mirror.

She said, "We're being followed."

The pair of headlights behind us were bright. High beams. The car was fifty yards behind us. Aurora put her foot down on the accelerator. The Renault stuttered forward.

We reached a long patch of straight road. The car behind us picked up its pace. Within seconds it was right up on our rear bumper. A dark-colored sedan, large and wide. If Aurora had slammed on the brakes they would've landed in the Renault's back seat.

"We can't outrun them," I said. I had to shout over the ruckus made by the Renault's engine rattling at top speed. I felt trapped and afraid inside that tin pot of a car. The machine gun still rested in my lap but I didn't think it wise to start waving it around inside the car.

I reached down and picked up the revolver instead.

Aurora looked scared. In the greenish glow of the dashboard lights and the brighter beams of light pouring in from the rear window I saw once again the fear in her eyes. She knew very well that we had little chance of escaping this latest threat.

The road wound to the left and then to the right. I turned in the seat and studied the headlights shining through the rear window. The sedan swerved left. A man in the passenger seat waved a pistol out of his open window as the sedan pulled out into the oncoming lane. They were preparing to pull up alongside of us. I shouted a warning. Aurora spotted them in her side mirror and she swerved into the oncoming lane as well, to cut them off and keep them behind us.

The sedan fell back a few yards.

We sped down the road in the wrong lane. I kept my eyes on the sedan and raised the pistol. Ready to fire through the rear window. Suddenly the inside of the Renault was full of sharp bright light cutting through the windshield. A transport truck had just appeared from around the curve ahead. It was heading straight for us.

A tremendous blast from the truck's air horn rent the darkness.

Aurora swerved back into the proper lane at the last second. With the sedan right behind us. I heard the dead grinding of the transport truck's brakes. The truck's running lights quickly receded as we sped on.

The sedan stuck with us.

Aurora said, "What are you waiting for?"

We entered another curve.

Aurora said, "Shoot out the headlights."

I aimed the revolver. I wondered what my chances were of actually hitting a headlight.

I pulled the trigger.

The revolver bucked in my hand. A patch of the rear window disintegrated.

The dark sedan fell back. Both headlights still blazing. It was anybody's guess what I'd hit, if anything. After a moment the sedan sped up again. Rushing up behind us, the high-beam lights almost blinding me. Then came an enormous jolt as the front bumper of the sedan hit the rear of the Renault.

The Renault veered to the right with the force of the impact. For a second we seemed to be in an uncontrolled drift. Aurora shouted curses as she struggled with the steering wheel, tried to keep the car from skidding off the road and into the trees. Finally she regained control and pulled the car into the center of the road, halfway into the oncoming lane.

I raised the pistol again.

I fired.

The shot took out another portion of the Renault's rear window. At that same instant the dark sedan swerved into the oncoming lane, trying to pull up beside us again. But with the Renault racing straight down the center of the road there wasn't enough room on either side to get next to us. The sedan slowed down, then disappeared from sight as we rounded a long curve lined by fences.

For a second I thought that the last shot had convinced them to leave us alone but no, we weren't that lucky. As we came out of the curve the headlights appeared behind us. They picked up speed and gained ground. They would begin shooting at us soon. There was no doubt of that in my mind.

I dropped the revolver between the two front seats and pulled the table cloth from the machine gun. I turned back toward the rear of the Renault and raised the gun. I had no idea what to expect when I pulled the trigger. Whatever happened, it would be loud and scary.

But before I could pull the machine gun trigger a gunshot came from the sedan. I heard the ring of metal hitting metal as the round lodged itself somewhere in the Renault's trunk.

Aurora shouted at me to get on with it.

I raised the machine gun again.

When I pulled the trigger a great burst of rattling erupted, and the gun kicked and bucked and almost jumped out of my hands. Cartridge casings flew past my cheek and shot across the front seat. Aurora took one hand off the wheel and raised it to deflect the hot brass casings away from her face.

The sedan swerved right. Then it fell back as the driver hit the brakes. The machine gun burst had certainly given them pause.

And I'd succeeded in hitting one of their headlights.

I glanced at Aurora. She lowered her chin and braced her arms against the wheel as she guided the car through a curve. The centrifugal force of the curve pushed me back against the door panel. I felt the warm barrel of the machine gun near my face, heard the Renault's wheels starting to slide on the surface of the road.

I was certain that we were going too fast. But somehow Aurora kept the speeding Renault on the road.

I looked behind us. The dark sedan was halfway through the curve that we had just navigated when I saw the vehicle begin to slide. The driver corrected for the slide and the sedan swerved back into the center of the road as it shot forward out of the curve. I could hear the roar of the sedan's engine clearly as the driver accelerated. There was a flash of light from the passenger side and then another flash. One of the gunshots put a large cobwebbed hole in the Renault's windshield. I pointed the machine gun and fired another wild burst. The inside of the Renault was full of the smell of burned gunpowder.

The sedan fell back. I'd knocked out the other headlight. But the driver was resourceful. He turned on a pair of fog lights that rested low along the front bumper of the sedan. They didn't give him a lot of light but it was enough. The passenger fired another two or three shots at us. Aurora shouted something, I don't know what. Madly I fired the machine gun, keeping my finger on the trigger until the clip was empty.

The sedan swerved toward the edge of the road just as we entered another curve. I'd hit something important. There was another flash of light from the sedan—another gunshot.

Then, just as the sedan seemed to drift smoothly off the road at high speed and crash into the darkness of the roadside behind us, the rear of the Renault jumped and kept jumping. The car pulled hard to the right and there was a pounding noise.

Aurora shouted. "We've lost a tire. Hang on."

Aurora fought with the steering wheel. Tried to keep the bucking Renault under control.

We slid out of the curve and kept sliding. In the headlights Aurora spotted a narrow dirt road on the left shoulder of the main road. The dirt road led out into trees and darkness. She spun the steering wheel and the Renault swerved off the main road and onto the dirt track, the back of the car swinging around. The car shook and bucked on the rutted surface of the road, like the machine gun had shook and bucked in my hands a moment before.

Aurora yanked hard on the wheel one last time and the Renault crashed through a wooden fence and tore through a hedge and bounced into a patch of tall grass.

The tall grass parted just as we ground to a halt.

The Renault had come to rest on the edge of a freshly plowed field.

Aurora turned the lights off. The engine had died on its own. After all the sound and fury of the last few minutes, the sudden silence was startling.

Aurora pushed her door open roughly.

"Last stop," she said. "Time to leg it."

16

Our legging was quickly curtailed. The soil in the field was freshly turned and uneven and, thirty yards in, Aurora lost her footing and fell. When she got up to run on she found that she couldn't.

She'd twisted her right ankle. The best she could do was a hobble. She wrapped her arm around my shoulders for support and I guided her forward, moving as fast as we could on my two good ankles and her one.

We struggled across the open field. It seemed to take hours. A break in the cloud cover left us in moonlight. I kept looking behind us. The car pursuing us had crashed, but that wasn't the end of it. Other pursuers were out there, somewhere.

Perhaps closer than we knew.

On the other side of the field we found more tall grass. We paused, out of breath. We had no idea where we were. The light from the moon disappeared above the clouds. There seemed to be a hillside in the distance, dotted by lights from scattered houses. We decided to traverse the hillside.

"Can you make it?" I said.

"I'll have to," Aurora said. "We can't stay here." A little curt about it. Like she didn't want to acknowledge her injury. Didn't want me to think that she was in any way unfit to carry on.

We stumbled through the grass in the darkness. Aurora's breathing sounded rough, or perhaps it was my own breathing. The ground began to rise. Soon we were moving uphill through a stand of trees. Both of us wore heavy sweaters but the night air cut right through them. Could we risk stopping at one of these scattered houses to ask for a lift into the next town? The chances seemed better that the locals would simply call the police. That wouldn't help us much.

"How are you doing?" I said.

"Hunky-dory," Aurora said, a little out of breath.

We reached a clearing and stopped and looked off into the darkness behind us, toward the paved road in the distance. We saw a pair of headlights passing on the road. The headlights didn't slow down. There was still no sign that anyone had followed us.

We hobbled farther up the hill.

After another twenty minutes we came close enough to a small house to see the floodlit driveway and a garage. Which meant there was some type of road nearby. We skirted the edge of the property and found an asphalt road leading up the hillside.

Walking on the asphalt was much less effort than walking across bare ground and we moved faster than we had before. A few hundred yards farther up the hill we came upon a pile of boulders beside the road and we stepped off the asphalt and walked up a short incline and sat down on top of the highest rock to rest. From our perch we could see the lights of the house we had just passed, below us on the hillside. In the distance we could see the headlights of the occasional vehicle traveling on the road to Marseille.

I said, "Does it hurt much?"

Aurora said, "It's sore. Let me catch my breath."

Right then we saw in the distance a pair of headlights slowing down on the main road. The headlights turned in the darkness, right where the dirt road should've been. The headlights came to a stop. Right about where the Renault mowed down the stretch of fence and hedge and fifty feet of tall grass.

The headlights went out. Another light appeared, not so bright. A flashlight. The beam of light moved off to the right of the dirt lane, following what might have been the trajectory of the Renault. Then it paused, at just about the spot where the Renault had come to rest. Aurora and I watched in silence as the light moved off in one direction for a few yards, then moved off into another direction, and then a third. Whoever was down there was looking for some clue as to where we had gone. But even if they found our footprints in the freshly-turned soil of the field, it wouldn't do them any good. We were well hidden now. They could search for us all night and never find us up here.

Or so we hoped.

After a few more minutes the flashlight beam returned to the dirt road and went out. The headlights came back on. The car sat there for a while, the occupants maybe engaged in a discussion. It had been forty-five minutes since we'd skidded off the main road. For all they knew we had flagged down a passing car and were ensconced in Montpellier or Aigues-Mortes by now.

The pair of headlights returned to the main road, then disappeared, heading east.

Aurora said, "I'm cold."

She moved closer. I put my arm around her shoulders and pulled her closer still. I felt the crown of her hair against my cheek. Her hair smelled of citrus. It felt soft like silk or satin.

She said, "We need to press on."

She didn't sound like she meant it.

"Let's give our friends in the car time to give up on us," I said.

She said, "I'm not so sure they will."

We sat on the boulder for a while longer. Watching and waiting and resting. Except for the occasional car or truck passing by on the main road the landscape below us remained quiet in the darkness. We huddled together to keep warm.

We talked to pass the time.

Aurora told me about herself. Bits and pieces. That her surname was Osman. That she was born in Algeria but her family had moved to the English Midlands when she was young. That she studied mathematics at the University of Edinburgh before returning to Algeria and then, finally, coming here to France.

"How does a woman who studied math in Edinburgh wind up cooking meals at a hotel in Sète?" I said. "Or was this the exact career ladder you envisioned."

Aurora shrugged. She tugged on her ear. A nervous habit, perhaps. "I wanted to return to the land I was born in. I lived first in Oran, and then later in a small resort area outside of Algiers called Pointe Pescade. I met a man there who worked for Ali El-Kef. The man became my husband and we came here to Sète to work. I am no longer married but I still work for El-Kef. Have you ever been married, Mister Slade?"

"Once."

"How was it?"

"Short."

"Tragically?"

"Mercifully."

Then I asked Aurora the question I had wanted to ask for quite some time. "What exactly did you know about the death of Monika Robichaux, or whatever her real name was?"

Aurora considered the question. She had told me a little about the incident in Nice last night at the hotel. But I wanted to know all of it.

Then Aurora began. "El-Kef sent me to Nice with three of his men. I wasn't told why, but that was not unusual. I stayed at a hotel in the Cimiez neighborhood. The next afternoon I was taken to El-Kef's boat—it was docked at Cap Ferrat. He gave me the memory stick and a description of you"—Aurora nodded at me, a note of apology in her voice—"and some clothes and a wig that I was told to wear. I put the disguise on and then I took a cab to the Musée on the Promenade in Nice.

"I walked to the café from there and made the contact and then I left. One of El-Kef's men picked me up and we drove around Nice for quite some time, I suppose to shake off anyone who might be following. Then he took me back to the hotel in Cimiez. The next morning he drove me back to Sète. I didn't know what it was about and I didn't ask. Ali El-Kef is not a man who explains himself."

"But you made a stop first, the next morning."

Aurora nodded again. "As we were leaving Nice we heard on the police radio that you had been located and we drove there, just to see what might transpire. That's when you saw me. But no one said that I was impersonating a Frenchwoman, alive or dead. Not to me."

The conversation drifted off into silence. Aurora had spoken haltingly of the events in Nice, as though she didn't quite believe them herself. As I had the night before, I wondered how much of what this woman told me I should credit. It was a question I couldn't answer, but the mere fact that I asked myself told me that I wanted to believe it.

Presently we climbed back down to the road and followed it around the side of the hill. Aurora walked unaided for a short distance, but I returned to her side to support her when she started to fall behind. I checked my watch. It was just past eight o'clock. To the best of Aurora's estimation, we were still nearly 60 miles from Marseille.

"Who is this person who can help us?" I said.

"A friend."

"What kind?"

"A friend who gets things done without a lot of bother."

"How much is the reward on my head?"

"I'm not aware of a reward."

"I must be worth something."

"Don't overestimate your value."

"Then why did you help me escape?"

Aurora raised her chin. Stared into the night ahead of us. She said she hadn't wanted to shoot the man in the hotel. But she'd had no choice. He'd have shot her otherwise. I told her not to trouble herself with guilt. She'd saved her own life and mine too.

She said, "I helped you because I feel that I owe you that much. Because of the other night in Nice, and the trouble you've gotten into. Not that I am in any way to blame for all of that."

"What part can I blame you for?"

"None of it."

"Then let's talk about the people we can assign blame to."

"All in good time, old boy."

We followed the road for another hour. Aurora's arm remained wrapped across my shoulders and progress was slow. Still, she believed her ankle felt better, and from time to time she put weight on it for short distances. "The name 'Rising Sun'—what does it mean?" I said at one point.

"I believe the name is a reference to the ancient Egyptians and one of their gods," Aurora said. "The organization's use of the scarab as a sort of calling card also ties back to historical Egypt."

I couldn't quite recall what a scarab was.

"The dung beetle," Aurora said.

I thought of the man in the cage. Ivashko. I saw again the tattoo on his arm. A rough tattoo of a cockroach, or so I had thought. I mentioned this to Aurora.

"What is the significance of dung beetles?" I said.

"If I remember properly, the dung beetle was a type of sacred object in ancient Egypt. The Egyptians believed that dung beetles were a worldly manifestation of the god Khepri. Khepri was also known as the god of the Rising Sun. It was believed by the Egyptians that Khepri rolled the sun into the sky every morning, then rolled it back into the twilight world of the gods every night. Dung beetles were associated with Khepri because dung beetles live on feces, which they sometimes roll into small balls and drag behind them."

"So the Egyptians equated the sun with a ball of shit."

"They were an earthy people."

"And a dung beetle looks like a cockroach."

Aurora shrugged. "A bug is a bug. Good for stepping on and not much else."

I thought again of the ambush in Nice. Why would members of a Russian criminal empire want to either rescue me from the clutches of the French police, or make sure that I was dead before I could talk extensively to anyone. I could think of no reason at all.

The Rising Sun was confused. Horribly confused.

As we came around a curve on the hillside road we caught sight of civilization. It started out as small patches of light in the distance, but after another half hour of walking it became a small village. A road sign indicated that we were now entering the environs of Deux Pistoles.

We walked into the village. The restaurants and shops we passed were dark and shuttered. In the center of the village, as we crossed an empty square, we heard the insistent bass thump of discotheque music. We followed the thunderous noise into a side street where a nightclub called Le Club Mexiko was open for business. Aurora went inside to use the phone. Walking with a pronounced limp, but under her own power now.

I remained on the sidewalk to keep a watchful eye on the street. Two young women in boots and short skirts, silvery spangles glued to their eyelids, stepped out of the club to share a cigarette. They whispered to each other, their arms folded tight and shoulders hunched against the cold. I saw no one else on the street. Then Aurora returned. She hadn't reached her friend in Marseille but she had succeeded in calling a local taxi. She thought she had woken the driver from a deep sleep but she wasn't sure. We became sure when the cab driver turned up in a white Mercedes a few minutes later. His curly hair was disheveled and he wore a pajama shirt under his denim jacket. But the prospect of a fare to Marseille seemed to excite him. Aurora handed him fifty Euros against whatever the trip would cost. The driver was so eager he tried to drive away before I'd climbed into the back seat.

17

We traveled on a country road for a while before reaching a secondary highway. We sped into the outskirts of Marseille thirty minutes later. In the old quarter along the waterfront the narrow streets twisted and turned and crisscrossed and cut back on themselves. It took some effort to find the bar where Aurora said she could meet up with her Marseille friend.

It was an English-style pub located in a cellar on a dark cobblestone side street, not far from the harbor. The sign hanging over the stone steps that led down to the entrance of the pub depicted a jovial porcine face wearing a bowler hat and black bow tie. A pint of foaming beer was hoisted impossibly in one pig hoof.

We had arrived at The Bourgeois Pig.

More Euros were placed in the cab driver's sweaty palm. Then the roar of the Mercedes echoed off the buildings as he sped off into the night. We heard raucous laughter floating up the stone steps from inside the pub.

"You friend works here?" I said.

"No, she doesn't," Aurora said. "But the bartender here will know where I can find her."

The pub was going full tilt. The tiny barroom was filled to capacity with customers quaffing beer or wine or the bright green absinthe that was served in pint glasses. One of the two bartenders was a stoop-shouldered man with a round flat nose that suggested he might be a distant relative of the pig on the sign outside.

Aurora pushed through the customers standing at the bar and spoke to the stoop-shouldered bartender. He leaned in close to catch every word. He nodded when she was finished, poured two pints of beer, then disappeared into a back room.

Aurora handed me one of the pints and sipped at the other. It was Guinness, black and viscous. I drank down half of the pint in one long gulp. It hit the spot. We had just finished the round when the bartender reappeared. He leaned across the bar and spoke to Aurora. She nodded and took two more pints and rejoined me.

We found a square inch or two of space near a narrow hallway at the rear of the barroom and we stood there and worked on the fresh beers. I felt the rush of alcohol warmth. Perhaps Aurora felt it too, because all of a sudden we were smiling at each other, like school children who'd just gotten away with a first-class prank. We had reached safety, if Aurora was to be believed. And I believed her. Why not? We were well-hidden, tucked away in a tiny English pub in the midst of the dark maze-like streets of Marseille's old port.

"Someone will be by to pick us up shortly," Aurora said.

"This all sounds a little shifty."

Aurora lowered her chin and gave me an up-from-under look. "Steady. Everything is shifty in Marseille. Be thankful that we found a cab in Deux Pistoles. We might still be wandering across the countryside."

We finished the second round and started in on a third one. The sense of relief from escaping the danger of the last few hours mixed with the alcohol and became light-headedness. I thought it might be wise to sit down. "Let's get a table." I looked around. There appeared to be another room down the narrow hallway. "Maybe in the back room."

Aurora didn't move. I noticed that her wry eyebrow was back at work. She said, "Did I tell you I wrote a poem once?"

"I don't think so."

"At the university. I called it 'Ode to a Cheeky Bastard.' It went, 'There was a hungry young lass from Loch Ness, who claimed Bangers and Mash were a mess—"

"Never mind."

"Bear with me."

"It looks dark."

"No, the ending is quite clever."

"The back room—it looks dark."

"Is there seating?"

"More or less."

Aurora hit me playfully on the shoulder. "How cruel of you."

"What?"

"You guessed the ending. Of my poem. 'But her beau wasn't blue, when the Spotted Dick wouldn't do, he slipped her a Toad in the Hole, more or less.'"

"You can explain it to me later."

"It got me high marks."

We pushed through the crowd and stepped into the back room. The patrons back there sat shoulder to shoulder on long benches at wooden tables. I could smell the sourness of a hundred years of spilled beer and wine that had soaked into the plank floor.

We found a seat at one of the tables. The raucous conversations of the people gathered at the table proceeded in four or five languages. Near me a drunk German was lighting a cigarette even though he already had a fresh one burning in the ashtray. His wife was adjusting her considerable cleavage with both hands. Across from them two French girls broke into song while a Greek man scratched himself and scowled. The air was a solid wall of cigarette smoke. A tray full of fresh glasses of beer and wine arrived and were fought over.

It was the perfect place to hide out.

I leaned in close to Aurora so that I could be heard above the general tumult. "Where did El-Kef go?"

Aurora glanced around the room before replying. As though afraid of being overheard. I don't know why. A small airplane could've crashed through the roof and I doubt anyone in the back room would have noticed, or would have cared much if they did notice.

"Back to Oran," Aurora said. "Or possibly Algiers."

"Won't the Rising Sun find him there too?"

"El-Kef knows Algeria the way other people know their living rooms. They'll never catch him."

"But he left you behind."

"He left a lot of people behind."

"What's going to happen to you?"

Aurora smiled. "You needn't worry on my account."

I turned to say something further to Aurora and noticed that she was studying a tall young man in a blue anorak who had just entered the room. He looked clean cut and strangely sober. She caught his eye and he came over. He leaned down and spoke into her ear. Aurora nodded and then turned and placed her hand on my shoulder.

She said, "Let's go."

I drank down the last of my beer and stood up. "No rest for the wicked."

We followed the man in the anorak out of the back room and down the hallway to the main room. We were halfway across the main room, pushing through the crowd on our way to the front door, when Aurora grabbed the back of the tall man's jacket and tugged on it hard. He stopped and turned and she said something hurriedly to him. Then he turned back around to look at the two men who had just stepped into the pub.

They stood together just inside the front door, studying the crowd. Both of them wore the flat expressions of hard men ready to take care of hard business.

They looked like the trouble we had been waiting for.

Aurora turned to me. "I've seen those two before. In Nice. The same night I ran into you."

"Do they work for El-Kef?"

"I don't know who they work for. And I don't want to find out."

But it was too late.

One of the men at the door had spotted Aurora. He nudged his friend and nodded in our direction. How many more thugs were waiting outside to grab us in the event that we slipped past these two and got out the door?

The tall man in the anorak turned. He looked past our shoulders at the narrow hallway we had just emerged from. "Perhaps there is a back way out," he said. He spoke English like an Englishman.

Aurora said, "The bartender would know."

It occurred to me that it was the bartender who had alerted the hard men to our presence in the pub. Who else knew who we were? "The bartender knows a little too much, if you ask me."

The Englishman said, "The bartender isn't a worry."

But the stoop-shouldered bartender was nowhere to be seen. We retreated a few steps farther back into the crowd. The two hard men kept an eye on us as they leaned in close to speak to each other. They were formulating a plan. Wading into the crowd to drag us bodily out of the pub probably wasn't an option. It would complicate things. Right now the one thing that we had in our favor was the thick crowd that surrounded us.

I took another step backwards and pulled Aurora back with me. The Englishman looked troubled. I glanced around the crowded barroom. The best thing for us was to simply stay in the pub, it seemed to me.

Then I saw our salvation.

In a dark corner of the pub.

A group of men sat there, around a café table that was covered with empty and half-empty pint glasses and over-flowing ashtrays. There were six of them and they were drunk. Bleary-eyed drunk. One of them sat with his head resting against the wall behind him, his eyes closed, his life-less hand still wrapped around a half-finished pint of beer. All of them wore mufflers or wool caps in the same red and blue color scheme.

They were the English football supporters who'd given me a ride from Antibes to Marseille the night before.

The Grunstead's Bittermen.

I wondered if they could stand up without falling forward

onto their drunken faces. I didn't wonder long. I grabbed Aurora's arm and pushed through the crowd toward the Bittermen's table. I had an idea and I needed her help to make it work.

The Englishman in the anorak watched our progress as he held his position in the middle of the barroom. As Aurora and I approached the table, the Bitterman called McBrain looked up. A half smile appeared on his face when he recognized me. The others looked around ponderously, as though they weren't quite sure where my voice had come from, or if they had only heard it in their heads. Slowly their faces turned toward me and then moved past me to Aurora.

"It's the Yank," McBrain said. The words were bent in odd ways as they came out of his mouth. "What we gave a ride to. And he's got himself a friend. Hello, my dear. What do you need a Yank for when you've got myself, one of England's finest, seated before you and ready to appease your every whim."

Aurora glanced at me. I nodded toward the men.

"Gentlemen, this is Aurora," I said. "From England."

"Hello, boys," Aurora said. She gave the seated Bittermen a high-wattage smile. "What's the news from Blighty?"

"The Yank found himself an English girl," McBrain said. He closed one eye to get a more focused look at Aurora. There was a murmur of approval among the other Bittermen. The one called Mickey Wedge tried to offer Aurora his chair, but when he stood up the chair fell backward and hit a Frenchman at the next table. The Frenchman turned his head and said something over his shoulder.

Mickey Wedge said, "*Vous vous trouvez drole?*"

The Frenchman said, "*Pissez.*"

The Frenchman brushed the underside of his chin with the backs of his fingers. He started to rise from his chair. Mickey Wedge placed his hands on the man's shoulders and pushed him roughly back down. The man thrust his arm back, trying to drive a sharp elbow into the Englishman's ribs. Then McBrain jumped up and pushed himself between his friend and the Frenchman. More words were exchanged. Somehow McBrain got Mickey Wedge back to his seat. Through the crowd I saw the Englishman in the anorak glancing uncomfortably back and forth between the two hard men at the door and Aurora and me at the Bittermen's table.

I turned back to the Bittermen and got to the point.

The six lads listened to me as well as they could as I explained that the two men at the door had followed us here from another bar. They had made a number of nasty remarks to Aurora and me about England and the Blackpool football team that was playing in Marseille the next day. They had even mistaken me for an Englishman and had challenged me to a fight. I made it clear to the Bittermen that I would have gladly taken on both of the hard men, were it not for the fact that I was worried for Aurora's safety.

Aurora tried to look hurt, but brave.

The Bittermen muttered to each other. Frowned. Peered through the holes in the crowd at the two hard men standing at the door.

"I think lessons need to be taught," McBrain said.

Mickey Wedge looked doubtful. "Are we paid up yet?"

Another of the Bittermen said, "We haven't paid."

Mickey Wedge smiled.

I laid it on even thicker.

"The bartender is a friend of mine," I said. "He also wants

those two out of here fast. I'm sure with the six of you and myself, we can make short work of it. And, of course, there wouldn't be any question of asking you to pay for your beverages. I owe you that much."

McBrain nodded. "Right enough."

Mickey Wedge raised his beer glass. "Down the gullet, mates."

Beer glasses were drained and slammed down on the table with decisiveness. The six Grunstead's Bittermen rose from their chairs. One of the quieter men pulled his British passport from inside his coat and held it up for the others to see. He shouted something in French. I didn't catch it but Aurora smiled.

"'*Honi soit que mal y pense*,'" she said, repeating for me what the man had just shouted. "It's on the cover of every British passport."

"What does it mean?"

"It's old French. It means, roughly, 'Shame to those who disparage Great Britain.'"

"Wonderful."

"You do seem to have hit the right note."

The six Englishmen began pushing none too gently through the crowd on their way toward the front door. McBrain and Mickey Wedge barked and howled like mad dogs. The other customers scrambled to get out of the way of this juggernaut of drunken Englishness. A general shouting arose. A pair of bookish middle-aged men stepped up to halt the advance of the Bittermen and restore order. They were brusquely pushed aside.

The two hard men now stood with their legs braced, arms hanging loose at their sides. Like boxers waiting for the fight bell to ring. The Bittermen surged forward toward them. A bystander caught up in the excitement threw a beer glass across the room. It hit the wall behind the bar and shattered.

Aurora's English friend appeared beside us. He shouted and pointed and told us to come along quickly. The stoop-shouldered bartender had returned. He was already disappearing into the hallway at the back of the main room with a ring of skeleton keys in his hand, and the three of us followed him past the back room and the restrooms until we came to a locked door.

The bartender worked a key around in the ancient lock. Behind us the commotion in the main room grew louder. The sound of glassware shattering was distinct. A chair bounced into the hallway and came to rest against an iron radiator just as several customers emerged from the back room carrying a wooden bench like a battering ram, ready to join the melee in the main room.

The bartender got the door unlocked. He pushed it open and stepped aside, motioning for us to move fast.

On the other side of the door was a wooden landing and a long flight of stairs leading down. Cardboard boxes and empty beer kegs were piled high on the landing. At the bottom of the flight of stairs was a door with a SORTIE sign on it and a crash bar to operate the latch. We raced down the trash-strewn stairs as best we could, Aurora starting out fast but slowing down when her bad ankle grew weak.

The door at the bottom opened onto an alley on a hillside, two stories lower than the street that ran in front of the pub. The alley was deserted except for an emaciated dog that watched us from a doorway. The Englishman looked around. Walked ten paces down the alley. Finally spotted what he was looking for. A small Citroen sedan, parked in a dark concrete stall that wasn't much larger than the car itself. The car belonged to the bartender, who had given the Englishman the keys.

The Englishman squeezed himself between the wall of the makeshift garage and the car. He somehow managed to get the door open and climb in behind the wheel. He started the car and pulled it out of the stall. Aurora got into the back and I took the front seat.

We rattled off down the alley in the Citroen.

"Where's the car you came in?" I said to the Englishman.

"Parked around front. Where the war that you started is now being waged. I'll return for it later. If it's still in one piece."

The Englishman didn't turn on the headlights until we reached the end of the alley and had turned onto a narrow street with a steep grade. We sped downhill, the cobblestones sending shudders through the car. The adrenaline that had pulsed through me only a few minutes ago was starting to recede. We had escaped a sticky situation and the relief inside the car was palpable.

"Another heroic chapter for British intelligence," the Englishman said. He let out a laugh that sounded like a snort. I laughed too. Thinking that the Englishman was making a reference to the collective IQ's of the drunken countrymen we had left behind in the pub. Then I heard a sharp intake of breath from Aurora in the back seat.

I stopped laughing. There was a long silence as I realized what the man had just said. He hadn't been making a joke about the English lads. He had said something else entirely. He hadn't said "British intelligence." He'd said "British

Intelligence."

I glanced at the Englishman. A sheepish look had fallen over his face. He pointedly kept his eyes on the road. He'd made a blunder. He'd thought I was in on the gag.

He was wrong.

The car reached the bottom of the hill. We rounded a curve and sputtered past a stone statue on a pedestal. I turned in the seat and looked at Aurora. Her face was half hidden by shadows. I could just make out the uncertain smile on her face.

She shrugged. Glanced out the window.

She said, "It keeps the bills paid."

18

I am a merchant of death.

For twenty years I sold death in various guises. I sold herbicides and rodenticides. I sold insecticides and avicides and fungicides and miticides. I aided and abetted the murder of entire strata of flora and fauna, around the globe. And I did it for money, nothing more and nothing less.

So why should I draw the line at homicide? Why should I voice displeasure over being dragged into some type of murderous conspiracy that involved a crazed Algerian smuggler, an international terrorist organization, and now the British Secret Intelligence Service? What qualms did I have any right to claim?

Nevertheless, qualms I had.

I was stunned and angry. The British Secret Intelligence Service—what the hell did MI6 want with me? As if it explained something, the Englishman driving the Citroen introduced himself as Alan Prescott-Browne. I assumed it was a cover name. I wondered what kind of bullshit intelligence operation I had stumbled across.

I tried to piece the bullshit together as we drove along

the narrow winding streets of Marseille.

If Aurora worked for Ali El-Kef and also for MI6, did El-Kef work for MI6 as well? But if that was the case, why would El-Kef run and leave Aurora behind? Was it part of a larger charade? And the dead Frenchwoman in Nice—was that the work of MI6 as well?

I asked all of these questions and a few more besides. Questions that existed in a murkiness that was thicker than any black Marseille night. Questions that I could feel like a hard blow to my spine.

My questions didn't get me anywhere.

"I know as little as you do," Aurora said.

"What about you?" I said to the Englishman.

He said, "I know even less than Aurora does."

"So no one knows anything."

The Englishman said to me, "You seem to know a bit." Then, "Save your questions. You'll be talking to Graham soon. She'll be able to help you."

"Who is Graham?"

"The person you'll be talking to soon."

I stared through the windshield of the Citroen. The questions buzzing in my head mixed with the whine of the Citroen's tiny 2CV motor. There were far too many questions and no answers and after a while I got tired of thinking about it.

We were outside of the city now. Rolling along a dark country road. The Englishman—Prescott-Browne—turned a knob on the dash and heat rushed out of the air vents. The hot air smelled faintly of gasoline. We rode for another few miles. Then he downshifted and guided the Citroen off the main road and onto a narrow dirt lane. A few yards farther on we stopped at an iron gate. The gate was closed.

A sign on the gate read:

LES FLEURS DES CALANQUES
Jardinerie
613 Route Jacques Soutine
13009 Marseille

Prescott-Browne got out of the car. He opened the gate and climbed back in and pulled the car forward, then got out again and closed the gate and returned to the car. We drove on. A house with a dark mansard roof appeared ahead. Floodlights lit the gravel-covered courtyard in front of the house. To the left of the house stood a large garage and, beyond the garage, I could just make out a long row of what appeared to be greenhouses, also lit by floodlights.

The Englishman pulled up in front of the house and Aurora and I climbed out. Then he pulled the Citroen into the garage and parked. Before the car's headlights went out I caught a glimpse of wheelbarrows and rakes and other garden implements. There was also another vehicle parked in the garage—a small delivery truck.

The house looked forlorn. The yellow paint on the window shutters was peeling and the white paint on the rest of the stucco house had worn away in large patches.

"MI6 seems to have come down in the world," I said to Prescott-Browne when he joined us on the porch.

He unlocked the door and pushed it open. "Don't jump to conclusions, Sunny Jim. You might fall and hurt yourself."

We stepped inside.

The interior of the house was as moth-eaten as the exterior.

A worn couch was positioned against a wall. It stood at an angle to a brick fireplace that had been painted white. A rocking chair and an overstuffed armchair sat on the opposite side of the fireplace and dim light came from an old lamp with a yellowed shade. The house smelled of lavender and boiled cabbage.

Prescott-Browne told us to wait there. He disappeared down a dark hallway. I heard knuckles rapping lightly on a hollow wooden door. Then the creak of door hinges, followed by a muffled conversation.

"You must be tired," he said to us when he returned. "Graham will talk to you in the morning. Would you like a spot of supper first?"

Aurora wasn't interested in food and neither was I. I was too tired to eat and too tired to think. Prescott-Browne led Aurora and me to a pair of bedrooms at the back of the house. The bedrooms were just large enough for a double bed and a narrow wardrobe. A soft glow from the floodlights that lit the greenhouses filtered in from outside through dormer windows.

Prescott-Browne left, then returned a few minutes later with a bottle of brandy and two snifters, which he set in the bathroom that connected the two bedrooms. He departed again without a word.

Somewhere in the house a furnace kicked on. I felt a rush of warm air from the floor vents. I stepped into the bathroom. It was nothing more than a sink with a counter big enough for the brandy bottle and the two glasses. Behind me was a narrow shower stall. But fresh towels hung on the towel rack, and the medicine cabinet held shaving cream, a razor, toothpaste, toothbrushes, and other common bathroom items. Had this Graham woman been expecting us?

I poured two brandies, then stepped out the other side of the bathroom and into Aurora's room.

She sat on the edge of the bed. She'd taken her boots off and she was massaging her sore ankle. I handed her one of the snifters and she took it and sipped at the brandy. She looked up at me from the bed.

"Is it any better?" I said.

"It's still a bit tender."

"Walking in those boots didn't do it any good."

"Thank you for helping me."

"Likewise."

"Are you angry with me?" Aurora took another sip of the brandy and then held the glass in both hands, as though warming her hands on the liquor. "If it matters, I don't actually work for MI6. I'm a sort of jobber. I keep an eye out and when I come across a situation I think they might be interested in, I send a report along. If they decide the information is of value, then they wire money into a bank account I keep in Sète. 'Funds from a relative in England.' It's all very low level. The only reason they're interested in me at all is because I work for El-Kef. He is always getting up to something with his smuggling and whatnot."

Aurora held the snifter up to her nose. She closed her eyes and breathed in the rich smell of the liquor. In the shadows thrown by the light from the bathroom she looked like a painting done in chiaroscuro. I said nothing. My anger at having been deceived once again was focused inward now. At my own general stupidity for getting involved in this mess.

"I'm going to take a shower," Aurora said. "Would you like to go first?"

"No, go right ahead."

"I won't be long."

I stepped into the bathroom and poured another finger or two of brandy into the snifter. Then I retreated to my own bedroom and closed the wooden sliding door behind me. The top of the door didn't quite reach the door frame and a sliver of light filtered into my room from the bathroom.

I sat on the bed and worked on the brandy, underneath the sliver of light. I heard Aurora in the bathroom. I heard faucets turning and the spray of water in the shower. I finished my brandy and sat the snifter on the floor and lay on the bed with my hands behind my head. The brandy eased into my veins like lullabies. Steam wafted into the room through the space at the top of the sliding door.

I fell asleep.

When I awoke it was still dark outside. The house was quiet and the light in the bathroom was off. I got up and slid the bathroom door open. The door on the other side was closed. I turned on the light. The brandy bottle was still there and I poured myself another drink. I wondered idly what would happen if I made a beeline for the front door and ran outside and disappeared into the night. Would Prescott-Browne chase after me in the Citroen? Perhaps he wouldn't bother. Perhaps he would stand at the front door and watch me run off and consider it good riddance to bad rubbish.

But the question was academic.

I had no place to run to.

I shaved, then undressed and climbed into the shower and stayed there until the hot water ran warm and then cold. I toweled off and brushed my teeth and stumbled back into the bedroom with my clothes under my arm. I finished the brandy and then climbed under the crisp sheets. I fell asleep again.

My dreams of the last few days had been vivid and had stayed with me after I awoke. Maybe it was a way of escaping the waking nightmare that I was trapped inside. This time I dreamt that I was out at sea. It wasn't the Mediterranean though. Someplace cold and rough. I stood on the deck of a ship. A hard wind blew across the choppy water. I was watching several men in a launch approach from a distant shore. There was ice on the deck and I stood with legs braced and my hands clamped tight on the gunwale railing. I heard an explosion and I turned. Smoke billowed from the pilot house. I tried to signal to the launch to stay back but it kept approaching on the white-capped waves. I was certain that they would die if they reached the boat. And I would die with them...

I woke up with a start.

Someone was in the room with me. I clenched my fist to strike out but I was still half asleep and I couldn't bring myself to let go of the ship railing that I had clung to in my dream. Then I smelled bath oils and felt long soft hair brushing against my chest.

I heard Aurora's voice.

"Steady, old boy."

I opened my eyes. I looked up. Daylight streamed in from the dormer window. It was morning and Aurora's face hung in the air above me. On one side of her face her hair was tucked behind her ear. On the other side it hung down straight and tickled my chest. She had burrowed under the blanket and now she straddled me. Her arms were braced against the mattress, on either side of my head. The smile

136

on her face was full of mischief.

I was reasonably certain that she had left her clothes in the other room. To test my hypothesis, I reached out and ran my hand down her back and along the contours of her round bottom.

Not a stitch.

"Wakey-wakey," she said.

She began humming as she leaned down and kissed my chest. If it was a tune she was humming, it was one that I didn't recognize. But my ignorance as to whether it was a tune or not did not trouble me. She raised herself up again. Looked into my eyes while I looked into hers. I started to say something, something that I hoped was suitably witty, but right at that moment Aurora arched her back and I found the business end of a dazzling breast pressed against my lips. I decided that it might be best, for the time being, to forego the conversational gambit and concentrate on the work at hand.

19

Prescott-Browne was seated at a farmhouse table eating breakfast when I walked into the kitchen. He invited me to fix my own meal. There were eggs and beans and slabs of ham in the refrigerator, he said. Might even be a piece of blood pudding.

It was almost noon.

I was eating my fry-up when Aurora appeared. She wore a heavy wool sock on her good foot. A cloth bandage was wrapped around the ankle of her otherwise bare right foot. She raised a wry eyebrow at me and then looked away. She said good morning to both of us and went about ignoring me and attending to her breakfast. It wasn't a bad act but I think it was lost on Prescott-Browne. He didn't seem concerned one way or another about what might have gone on in the back bedrooms over the last hour. I wondered how well sound traveled in this house and decided I didn't care.

"When do we see Graham?" I said to Prescott-Browne.

"She's out checking on the roses. There was a frost on the ground this morning and the space heaters in the greenhouses are a bit dodgy."

the back in a loose chignon but bristly strands had worked free. She brushed the strands of hair off her forehead. "We knew it couldn't last."

"They were in civilian clothes—the men who came for him," Aurora said. "I don't think they were police."

"It might have been men from the Central Directorate," Graham said.

The Central Directorate? I had no idea what this old woman was talking about. I started to introduce myself. The woman waved her hand to indicate that an introduction wasn't necessary. Unaccountably I felt sheepish, like I was meeting Aurora's mother socially for the first time. Graham's eyes drifted off but the hand remained in the air. I wondered if I was expected to kneel and kiss it. The prospect of this woman being an MI6 operative seemed unlikely in the extreme.

The old woman sensed my doubts. The waved hand drifted back down to the arm of the chair.

"Have no fear, Mister Slade. We are quite capable of getting you to a place of safety. You of all people should understand at things are not always as they appear."

"You can say that again."

"I don't need to." She puckered her lips as she considered thing. Then, "Mister Slade, right now I want you to tell rything that has occurred since you arrived in France. oing to help you, I need to know every detail of your lations."

is it you plan to do?"

kles on Graham's face rearranged themselves into lan to keep you alive. At least long enough to gland."

glish."

"That's not germane."

"It is for me."

Graham sighed. "Very well." She leaned forward. Reached down into the wicker knitting basket that rested on the floor next to the chair. Her hand slipped under a pile of balled yarn and felt around, then reemerged, holding a large automatic pistol. She pointed the pistol at me. Her hand was steady. So was the look in her eyes.

Graham gave me a strained smile. "I find that the presence of a firearm tends to keep the conversation focused. Wouldn't you agree?"

I didn't answer. After a moment Graham laid the pistol in her lap, the barrel pointed in my direction. The look in her eyes remained hard. "Mister Slade, it might interest you to know that I was shooting rebels in Kenya for Her Majesty's Government when you were still suckling at your mother's teat." Graham paused to give Aurora a distasteful look. Aurora's expression fell. Graham said, turning back to me, "I've dispatched men to the great beyond who were much more dangerous than you. More handsome too. And it hasn't bothered me in the slightest. I sleep soundly at night. So do please reconsider your recalcitrance. I can assist you in your escape, but only if you can help me with my inquiries."

An awkward silence followed. It was broken finally by the whistle of a tea kettle. A minute later Prescott-Browne returned from the kitchen. He carried a silver tray set with a cup of steaming tea on a saucer, a tiny pitcher of cream, a spoon, and what looked like small shortbread cookies arrayed on an *hors d'oeuvre* plate. He set the tray on the lamp table next to Graham's chair, then moved off to stand against the wall near the kitchen doorway. Like an attentive servant should.

"Tell me about the Central Directorate first," I said to Graham. "Who are they and what do they want?"

Graham sighed. She explained that the Central Directorate—more properly, the *Direction Centrale du Renseignement Interiéur*—was a pale imitation of Great Britain's MI5. "In matters of terrorism, the National Police take their orders from the Central Directorate. We've heard things in the past few days that seem to suggest that the DCRI has taken an interest in El-Kef's operation, but the situation is still evolving. And how exactly you fit into this"—the old woman nodded at me—"is very much open to speculation at the moment.

"Now let's get on with it, Mister Slade," Graham said.

Graham waved us over to the couch and Aurora and I sat down. I was on pins and needles. A pistol had been brandished and oblique threats had been made. And yet Graham said that she wanted to help me. She had a curious way with people, that much was clear. But maybe she did want to help. I couldn't afford not to hear her out. I didn't have so many options.

While Graham worked on her tea I tried to tell her what she wanted to know.

It seemed like a hundred years ago. I walked into a cafe in Nice and sat down. A woman came in and sat down next to me. Pressed the barrel of a gun into my side. Left me with a flash drive. Disappeared out the back. A man with a skull for a face stepped inside, looked around, then departed. It all seemed so distant. Like it had happened in another life. Graham listened carefully as I recounted the tale. Sipping her tea. Nibbling at a shortbread cookie. She interrupted me only to clarify a fact here and there. Her eyes were sharp and penetrating. I had the feeling that I was being debriefed.

That everything I said was going to wind up in a classified report carried in a diplomatic bag to London. Under the circumstances, that scenario didn't seem like much of a stretch.

I felt Aurora's hand on mine when I was finished. She wanted to reassure me.

Graham brushed shortbread crumbs off the front of her sweater. "Mister Slade, what I can do for you is this," she said now. "Once we get you to England, I can offer you the protection that comes with hiding in plain sight. You must speak with our contacts at the British newspapers and at the BBC. Get your story out into the public eye. You must, in short, maintain a high level of visibility. If you stay in the shadows, you will be killed."

"Who is it that wants to kill me?"

"Your own people."

"I don't have 'people.'"

"Your friend Morgan, for one."

There was a long silence. The idea that Septimus Morgan wanted me dead was ludicrous. So ludicrous that I didn't bother to argue the point. Graham watched me closely. Studying my reaction. I stared back at her. We were playing a game of who-blinks-first. She didn't blink. I smiled and turned to Aurora. She wasn't smiling.

"It is no laughing matter, I can assure you," Graham said. "Septimus Morgan works for your country's Central Intelligence Agency. He has done so for many years. Does that surprise you? Mister Morgan has made himself known to us on a number of occasions in the past. He disappeared for a time and we thought we had done with him. We were quite surprised to learn recently that he is still on the job. He is an *agent provocateur*, Mister Slade. He engages in what I believe in your country are called 'dirty tricks operations.'"

The smile on my face was still there but now it was pasted on like a mask. I said the only thing that came to mind.

"You're a crazy old bat, aren't you."

"We can discuss the state of my faculties later, if you wish," Graham said, shaking her head. "Right now you must understand that Septimus Morgan wants you dead."

20

The conversation had taken a giant step into the absurd. I wasn't sure I wanted to go with it. But I kept talking to buy myself time. Time to think. Time to consider what this woman truly wanted from me. Graham shifted in her chair and picked up another shortbread cookie. She chewed the cookie and fixed her gaze once more on me.

I said to Graham, "What reason would Morgan have to kill me?"

"There has been a bit of a ruckus in the French press in recent weeks," Graham said after a pause. "Perhaps you've heard. Allegations of chicanery and whatnot have been leveled by the French government against the intelligence services of Britain and America. What the French media hasn't spoken of is that MI6 and the CIA are both working toward a common goal—the capture of international terrorists who have operated quite freely on French soil. One of the organizations involved is one you have already encountered—the Rising Sun.

"The French, of course, don't believe the terrorists are active here. They are uniquely thick-skulled in these matters. The

145

most efficacious way to force the French government to face ugly truths is to bring the current situation to a boiling point. My government has chosen to do this through diplomatic channels and a gentle prodding. Your government, Mister Slade, hoping to gain the upper hand, has chosen to do this through the channel it knows best—base manipulation and lies.

"Shake your head if you must. It won't change the truth of this. The Rising Sun has posed problems not only for my government but also for yours. The organization is making alliances with other terrorist groups throughout the Middle East and Asia. The Al-Qaida organization is the most visible of these organizations, but there are several others that may come to prominence shortly.

"Recently we learned from sources inside the French National Police that a known operative of the Rising Sun, a man named Fyodor Grunikov, would be visiting Nice. Our information told us that he was coming here to purchase information that, in the wrong hands, could be dangerous indeed."

I recalled the newspaper article I'd read in Sète. "The plans for a high tech laboratory to make mustard gas."

"Quite right. Mustard gas. A somewhat antiquated approach to bio-terrorism, but an effective one. The plans were stolen from a British Ministry of Defense plant in Cornwall last year. Through a somewhat circuitous route they wound up in the hands of a French national named Monika Robichaux."

I recalled the dark photograph of the Frenchwoman's body lying in a garbage-strewn alley. "She was murdered in Nice."

A look of regret crossed Graham's face as she raised a finger to wipe an errant cookie crumb from the corner of her mouth. I wasn't sure if she regretted the death of the woman in Nice, or the presence of the crumb. She went on. "We'll get to that presently. Try to follow this, Mister Slade. We learned through our electronic surveillance of Rising Sun assets in Prague that the purchase was to be made in Nice on a particular date. We proposed to notify the French police of what was about to occur, so that they could monitor the drop. In that way we could prove to them once and for all that the Rising Sun was operating quite freely right under their quivering Gallic noses. Our surveillance told us one other thing—Grunikov didn't know Mademoiselle Robichaux. He had only the roughest description of the woman he was to meet.

"But what we did not know was where in Nice the drop was to take place. In order to further our cause we contacted Ali El-Kef and asked for his assistance. He was directed to intercept Monika Robichaux when she arrived in Nice, learn from her where the drop was to happen, obtain from her the computer memory stick that contained the information, then substitute another woman to make the drop. We couldn't risk doing it ourselves, for obvious reasons. But El-Kef was game and he agreed to help us—for substantial emoluments, of course.

"We were further encouraged in our endeavors when we learned that El-Kef had asked Aurora to help stage our little drama. As you must know by now, Aurora has also helped us in the past. Without El-Kef's knowledge. When you lie down with dogs, Mister Slade, it is helpful to know where the fleas are beforehand. Aurora has been quite useful to us in that regard."

I said, "So El-Kef does work for MI6."

147

Graham pursed her lips as she constructed a judicious answer. "He's not on our payroll, if that's what you mean to ask. Mister El-Kef is a professional smuggler. He sells to whoever is buying. At various times he has worked for us, for the Americans, for the Central Directorate, and god knows who else. He has ties to the usual underworld organizations and, no doubt, to the Rising Sun. I'm afraid that in our haste to gain his assistance in the matter of Grunikov and the mustard gas documents, we may have neglected to mention that the organization we were asking him to help us entrap was the Rising Sun. That may have been a tactical error on our part."

A tactical error. That was an understatement of the first order. The British had hired a smuggler to help them entrap a criminal network that he may have on occasion worked for. I recalled how El-Kef had acted in Sète. Confused. Erratic. Crazed. A man on tenterhooks. A man who could already hear the bullet coming, the one with his name on it.

I said, "What happened in Nice?"

"That is a bit murky at the moment," Graham said. "What we know for certain is that on the evening before the day of the scheduled exchange with Mademoiselle Robichaux, Grunikov suffered a heart attack in his hotel room. He died *en route* to the hospital. Needless to say, that threw a rather large spanner into our operation.

"But El-Kef was already at work. He intercepted Mademoiselle Robichaux the next morning, as planned, and detained her. After speaking with her persuasively, he learned where the drop was to occur. Robichaux had also been in touch with her Rising Sun contact that very morning, and she was able to inform El-Kef of Grunikov's untimely passing, and of the man being sent by the Rising Sun to replace Grunikov and go through with the planned drop. Robichaux admitted to El-Kef that she had never met the replacement, just as she had never met Grunikov.

"So, we were back on track. We notified our National Police contacts at the Central Directorate that we had learned through channels of the scheduled rendezvous. We also dispatched two of our own people to watch over the proceedings and take pictures, in case the French failed us. Then Aurora was put in Robichaux's place and, when she arrived at the café, she found you there. You fit the description she had been given of Grunikov's replacement, so she left the memory stick with you. Somewhat forcibly, I'm told. Then she left the café and El-Kef's men spirited her out of the area before the police could pick her up.

"In the event, the National Police performed their own surveillance. Unfortunately, there was a wrinkle to their activities that we weren't quite prepared for."

Graham paused to take a sip of tea.

"What sort of wrinkle?" I said. I glanced at Aurora. She hadn't said a word so far.

"You, Mister Slade, are the wrinkle," Graham said. "You were not the substitute for Grunikov that El-Kef reported to us. Which can only mean one of two things. Either El-Kef was misled about the new contact by Robichaux. Or El-Kef himself misled us. I'm inclined to believe the latter.

"In short, I believe that for reasons unknown to us, Mister El-Kef was paid by your Mister Morgan or his associates to queer the pitch, so to speak. Ali El-Kef was advised to pass on a description of Grunikov's replacement that fit you, Mister Slade. Your Mister Morgan knew you would be in

Nice that evening and he decided to use you as his stalking horse. That way, when the French police picked you up, they would not find the evidence of a Rising Sun operation that we very much wanted them to find. They would find evidence only of a dark plot hatched by the British and played out by an unknowing dupe. It has put us in bad odor with the French, and given the Americans a rather large edge in influencing French domestic security policies. Why Mister Morgan would put you at risk, I could not say. But, at the moment, I can only conclude that he now wants you out of the way.

"Of course, to make his ploy truly work, Mister Morgan must also show the French that El-Kef was in our employ. And to do that effectively, Morgan needed to double-cross El-Kef and turn him in to the police as well. That may explain the incidents in Sète yesterday. Although I have to believe that Morgan would much prefer to have El-Kef killed too. Which is where your man in the cage comes into play."

"Ivashko?"

Graham waved her hand dismissively. The man's name was of no consequence. "I suspect that you are mistaken about his affiliation with the Rising Sun. A better theory would be that he was hired by Morgan to liquidate El-Kef, and was caught as he tried to carry out his orders."

Graham seemed to have a pat answer for everything. Almost too pat. But there was one important question that she hadn't addressed.

"The ambush in Nice—who was behind that?"

Graham cocked her head to one side. An eyebrow curved up into a question mark and a faint clicking sound came from her mouth. The kind of sound that badly-fitted dentures make.

"I do not yet know the answer to that question," she said. "We are inclined to believe that it was the CIA. Think about it, Mister Slade. Who desperately wants you dead? I'm not sure the Rising Sun cares enough about you to risk a daylight ambush in the center of Nice. That is, if the Rising Sun even knew who you were at that point. But your friend Morgan and the CIA most assuredly want you on hiatus. On a somewhat permanent basis. Before you can say anything that might lead back to them."

"But I don't know anything."

Graham shrugged her shoulders. "You know Septimus Morgan. And that, I presume, is enough. You have been used, Mister Slade. You are a hapless tool. And now it is my good or bad fortune to pull the strings that will keep you out of the soup. Since you so obviously can't do it yourself."

I couldn't argue with Graham on that point. It was true. I had told Morgan where I would be staying. And I'd told no one else. I was a simple business traveler, arriving from Budapest. A man with few ties and fewer obligations.

Then a glimmer of understanding appeared. I tried to grasp it firmly. "If you've told me anything, Graham, it's that you're in a bad spot," I said. "The National Police think you purposefully tried to sell them a bill of goods. The only way out for you is to prove to them that you didn't. And you're going to use me to do that."

Graham set the teacup and saucer down on the tray. Wiped at her mouth with a napkin. "Is that such a bad thing, Mister Slade? Let me see now, how many people are rushing to your aid at the moment? Oh dear, exactly none. Other than myself. The French police want to throw you in a cell and leave you there until they get around to hanging you. The CIA wants you dead so that you can't put the lie to whatever rigmarole they are feeding to the French. And, quite possibly by now, the Rising Sun would like the pleasure of removing certain of your vital organs and shipping them by overnight post to Washington D.C. If I may be so bold, Mister Slade, I would suggest that you take what aid and comfort you can find, wherever you can find it."

Graham clapped her hands together as though the matter had been decided, she would brook no further argument. "We must get you to England. We must show the French and all of Europe what has gone on here. Are you prepared to look past your nationality so that the world may learn the truth?"

I looked again at Aurora. She was staring into the shadows behind Graham, no doubt wondering what fate was in store for her. I had fallen in with a fine bunch of civil servants. The hope that I could get back to the States soon appeared more and more remote.

Perhaps getting to England was a viable alternative.

But one question remained.

I said, "Graham, did you tell the French police that the flash drive that Aurora passed to me contained information on the manufacture of mustard gas?"

Graham shook her head. "It was important that they find out on their own."

I reached down and unlaced my left shoe. Pulled it off my foot. It was the shoe with the hollowed out heel that I often carried emergency cash in. I had taken the money out of the shoe in Nice. It had been the end of the trip and I was low on Euros. At that same time, as a simple precaution, I had wrapped the flash drive up in the plastic that had contained the paper money and inserted it into the hollowed out section of the shoe sole. It had fit there snugly.

Now I removed the blue and white flash drive from the shoe and unwrapped it from the plastic and held it up for Graham to see.

"This is the flash drive that Aurora passed to me in the café," I said. "It occurred to me that it might be important enough to keep hidden. Until I knew what it was and what to do with it. That's how it ended up in my shoe."

Graham peered at me. "Then you didn't give the police a memory stick?"

"I gave them one. But it was one that belonged to me. The only file on it was a manuscript for a book of poems that I wanted to discuss with Morgan."

"A book of poems?" Graham leaned forward and stared at the flash drive in my hand. She looked alarmed at first. Then a smile bloomed on her aged face. She sat back, her hands gripping the armrests of the chair. A small laugh like a cluck escaped from her mouth. "How terribly droll, Mister Slade. And would you like to hear something else that is droll? The information on that memory stick isn't worth a toss. It is technical data that could've been pieced together from any number of unclassified sources. We made sure of that. We had Monika Robichaux under surveillance in England well before she came into possession of those plans. She was duped, Mister Slade. Just as you have been."

21

I studied the tiny blue and white device in my hand. The National Police knew what the information contained on the flash drive was supposed to have been. And they didn't get it from me. What did that tell me? I wasn't sure. My reasoning processes were getting as balled up as the story Graham was telling. But I tried to imagine the moment when Inspector Brissac of the National Police or one of his men opened up the file on the flash drive to find nothing but long patches of my finely-hewn doggerel.

Droll, indeed.

I tossed the flash drive to Graham. She caught it adeptly.

I asked Graham what exactly she knew about Morgan. Graham finessed the subject. She made a dark reference to an MI6 asset based in Karachi who was killed on Lake Como in a suspicious boating accident two years before. A few months before his death the man had associated with Morgan in Istanbul, and Graham believed that Morgan had wanted the MI6 man out of the way in order to protect lucrative inroads Morgan had made within the Pakistani underworld. Graham said all this as though it proved something, but it proved nothing to me. When I asked for further details Graham waved me off, told me that it was all "hush-hush." It sounded more like bullshit to me. Morgan was no more a rogue CIA operative that I was the King of Siam. But the fact that Graham knew Morgan and knew of his association with me was troubling enough.

My thoughts returned to the Frenchwoman.

"Maybe your people killed Robichaux," I said to Graham. Just to see how she reacted.

The old woman flinched. Her hand fluttered in the air. "Oh dear me, no. We intended to turn Robichaux over to the police. That was why the disguise was involved. It wasn't an exceptional piece of stagecraft, but in a surveillance photograph taken at night Aurora would have looked enough like Robichaux to make it stick. Anything Robichaux could have said to the contrary once the police picked her up would have been useless. When all is said and done, Mademoiselle Robichaux was guilty as charged. We were merely forcing her hand."

Graham set the flash drive on the serving tray and tucked the pistol back under the balls of yarn in the wicker basket. She rose stiffly from her arm chair and clasped her hands together.

"Mister Slade, we need to get you to the airplane," Graham said. "I'll see what I can arrange. In twenty-four hours or so you'll be in London, talking until you are blue in the face with men in expensive suits who will not have the faintest idea how to resolve this problem. But at least you won't be here. I'll place a call to Bluebird directly."

I said, "'Bluebird?'"

"Our man in Lyon—where your flight will depart from."

155

I said, "What about Aurora?"

"I'll be fine," Aurora said. "I have an uncle in Cerbère. On the Spanish frontier. He has a boat and he can take me to Tangier, where my grandfather lives. I can stay in Tangier until things cool down. Then I'll go back to Sète and see if I can pick up where I left off."

"Preposterous," Graham said. "You can't go back to Sète."

Aurora sounded determined. "It wouldn't be wise for me to simply disappear. I have relatives still living in Algeria. I wouldn't want El-Kef to make things hard for them because he thinks I informed on him. If I run off, he will believe that I did."

"Nonsense," Graham said. "Let's get you to England. This situation is much too fluid to be safe for you or for any of us. As things stand, I wouldn't be at all surprised if Brownie and I are ordered to pull up stakes and scarper for the Home Counties ourselves within the next few days."

Aurora shook her head. "I can't."

The old woman gave Aurora a soft smile. "Graham knows what's best, my dear."

Aurora and I spent the rest of the day in the house. Graham and Prescott-Browne didn't believe it was wise for us to go outside, in case the property was under surveillance. Graham disappeared into a back room to contact London and Lyon by computer and make arrangements for our "exfiltration," as she called it. Meanwhile, Aurora and I monitored the news channels. We didn't learn much. The raid on El-Kef's operation in Sète wasn't mentioned. Which told us that it was an arm of the French Central Directorate that had staged the raid, as Graham had suggested. Only a high-level intelligence agency would have the clout to keep that kind of operation under wraps. In the name of national security, no doubt.

Around four o'clock the sky turned dark with storm clouds. A thunderstorm cracked the sky toward six. Dusk came and went while it rained hard outside. It was a toss-up as to which was blacker—the weather outside or our own thoughts.

Aurora and I had just eaten a light supper of cold pork and beets when Graham appeared in the kitchen.

She asked me to join her in the den.

The only light in the den came from two ancient wall sconces and the screen of Graham's computer. I sat down at the wooden table that she used as a desk. She stood beside me and turned the computer toward me. On the screen was a photograph of a middle-aged man walking along a city street on a sunny day. The photograph meant nothing to me.

"Are you sure?" Graham said.

"I've never seen him before."

Graham reached down and took hold of the computer mouse. She moved the cursor to one corner of the screen and then clicked the mouse. A new image appeared. Another photograph. Another man that I had never seen before.

"We are patched in to London," Graham said. "These are pictures of known or suspected operatives of the Rising Sun. I would like for you to study each photograph carefully. Take your time."

The quality of the images varied wildly. Some of them were stark black and white, others were in vivid color. Some were grainy and some were quite clear.

For ten minutes I shook my head at every picture.

Then one came up that startled me.

It was a photograph of a man sitting at a table outside of

a café. A half empty glass of beer and a folded newspaper lay on the table. Next to the glass was an ashtray with the word ALSACIENNE visible on the side. The color picture was clear and crisp. It looked like a holiday snapshot. The man wore a black polo shirt. His thin mouth was pulled to one side in a half-frown and his nose was flat and crooked. As though someone had once stepped on his face, then tried to grind his nose down the way one might grind out a cigarette butt with the heel of a shoe. The skin on his face was drawn tight and his eyes were dark and deeply set. It was a disturbing, skull-like face. And one that I had seen twice before. First at the Café Alcazar in Nice. And the second time in a Nice street, pulling a bloody wool ski mask from his head after he was wounded in the gun battle with the police.

Graham said, "You recognize that one, do you?"

I told her where I had seen him before. "Who is he?"

Graham leaned forward to study the picture. I caught the lavender scent of her perfume.

"Verga," she said. Her forehead was wrinkled in an expression of mild surprise. She moved the cursor to a small panel to the left side of the computer screen and clicked. A small white box appeared. Inside the box was the man's name and a brief summary of his background:

VERGA, ARNIK KONSTANTIN. *Greek-Romanian. Presumed active, Rising Sun Organization. Skilled marksman, student of Asian martial arts. Fluent Greek, Romanian, Italian, French, Khe Swahili. 1962: Born Athens, Greece. 1982—1987: Military Service, Greek Armed Forces, Paratrooper...*

The description of Verga's wanderings that followed

158

was terse, but suggestive. In 1998, Verga was implicated in the murder of a Russian physicist in St. Petersburg while attempting to sell stolen materials from a defunct nuclear facility near Riga, Latvia. Verga was also suspected of involvement in the 2005 murder of the British scientist and MI6 advisor David Kelly in Longworth, Oxfordshire, England, which may or may not have been related to Kelly's biological weapons studies in Iraq following the 2003 invasion by the United States, Great Britain, and supporting forces. More recently, Verga was implicated in the torture and murder of two Swedish journalists in Nairobi, Kenya.

"Verga is a monster," Graham said when she finished reading. "He's a rabid dog that needs to be put down. I recall the intelligence reports on the murder of the Swedes. They were tied together with rope, badly beaten, then dragged behind a Land Rover for several miles before being shot in the head at close range. Their bodies were largely eaten by hyenas before the remains were discovered."

But the one fact that stuck in my mind appeared in the first line of the synopsis. *Presumed active.* In less strained circumstances I might've laughed. There was no presumption about it.

Verga was very much on the job.

Graham clicked the mouse. The dialogue box disappeared. The image of Verga filled the screen again. Graham studied it a while longer. "We've reviewed the image intel that was collected in Nice that night," she said. "Verga's name has not come up. It's possible that we made a mistake. But it is more likely that you are mistaken."

"It's the same man."

"Very well, Mister Slade. Let's say for the moment that

you are correct. But that's all the more reason to get you out of the country *posthaste*."

"Would Verga follow me to London?"

Graham gave me a hard look. "If he has been directed to kill you, my sense of things is that Verga would follow you to the ends of the earth. But perhaps we can find that devil before he finds you."

Graham showed me several more photographs, but I recognized none of the individuals pictured. Finally Graham closed the computer file. I left the room with the image of Verga burned into my mind and Graham's remark ringing in my ears.

He would follow you to the ends of the earth...

The storm had subsided, leaving a light rain behind. The shadows inside the house grew deep. Prescott-Browne built a fire in the fireplace, then retired to the kitchen to work a crossword puzzle. He directed us to keep the curtains closed and to avoid turning on more lights. Best not to give the impression of a lot of activity inside the house. I sat with Aurora on the couch in the living room. She was eating Vichy Mints and reading a historical novel that she'd found. She rested her legs across my lap. The bandage on her ankle was loose and I rewrapped it.

We didn't say much. We shared the silence.

I stared into the flames in the fireplace. I saw Verga's face. The side of his head bloodied. Then I saw Morgan's face. The way I saw him last. Smiling. Jovial. Mixing drinks and telling me an amusing story about a writing assignment that had turned into a wrestling match. Talking and laughing. His wife Cordelia sitting beside him, throwing him dubious looks and laughing too as the vodka tonics kicked in and the stories became more complicated, more ribald. Had he made up those tales for my benefit? Were they all part of a script that was meant to hide his true occupation from outsiders like me?

And I certainly felt like an outsider. Profoundly. It seemed that everything I had ever thought was true was now in question. The rational world that I had lived in all of my life had suddenly shown its true colors. It wasn't rational at all. It was built on chaos and fear and death and lies. That I would disappear, and leave behind no evidence that I had ever been here, struck me right then as the only inescapable truth.

The weight and repetition of these thoughts was too much. I couldn't bear the company of my own mind. I told Aurora that I was tired. I went to the bedroom and washed up under the soft glow of the nightlight. I felt exhausted. But as soon as I lay down in bed my mind began racing again in the darkness of the room. I saw Morgan laughing. El-Kef screaming. The caged man whimpering. Verga pulling his bloodied cap off his head. Again and again and again. Then a new thought came to me. What if Verga's head wound had been mortal? Was it possible that Verga was dead? Once that thought appeared I couldn't let go of it. I wanted to believe it. I wanted it to be true…

I heard the bathroom door sliding open. In the soft glow of the bathroom nightlight I saw Aurora step into the bedroom. Naked except for her underpants. Holding one arm across her breasts as though afraid for her modesty. She slipped under the blanket without a word. I pulled her closer. For the next hour or so any thoughts of assassins and death were held well in abeyance.

22

It was still dark when I awoke. I heard a knuckle rapping on the bedroom door. Then Prescott-Browne's voice, giving me a wake-up call. He directed me not to turn on any of the overhead lights.

I rolled over. Reached out for Aurora.

She wasn't there.

I heard the water running in the shower.

Half an hour later we all met up in the kitchen. The room was cold and the only light came from a flashlight with a red translucent cap over the lens. The flashlight stood on its base on the kitchen table. It looked like a warning beacon.

Aurora handed me a mug of coffee and a plate of crackers and sliced cheese. Prescott-Browne leaned against the sink counter with his arms folded. Graham sat at the table drinking tea and nibbling at slivers of sliced apple. She wore a white boiler suit with the name of the nursery stitched over the breast pocket. There were two more boiler suits draped over the back of a kitchen chair.

"Put those on," Graham said to Aurora and me. "You'll find that they have their uses. I've arranged your flight out of the country but we have a long drive ahead of us. It would be wise to use the restroom before we leave. If you feel the need."

I handed Aurora one of the suits and took the other. We stepped into them and pulled them up and zipped the front.

"Where are we going?" I said to Graham.

"A private airfield outside of Lyon."

The flashlight was turned off and the four of us moved into the darkness of the living room. Prescott-Browne slipped outside, leaving the front door ajar. Graham whispered that it wouldn't do for all of us to go stumbling outside in the dark and make a ruckus that could be heard for miles. Better to let Prescott-Browne go out alone and make the preparations for our departure.

We waited. It was a quarter after six o'clock. The November dawn wouldn't appear for a good while. As we stood in the darkness I wondered if Graham had solid reasons to think the house was being watched. Or was it just caution born from years of hard experience with the Secret Intelligence Service?

I heard the creak of rusted hinges outside. Then a steady rustling, as though a pile of leaves was being kicked around. After a moment the dark outline of Prescott-Browne appeared in the doorway.

"Right as rain," he said.

Aurora and I stepped outside. Graham followed, pulling the door closed silently and locking it.

We made our way to the garage. In the distance I saw the glow of the floodlights that illuminated the greenhouses. A ground fog had moved in and the light looked diffuse.

We entered the garage through a side door.

Inside the garage Prescott-Browne turned on the capped

flashlight that he'd brought from the kitchen. We followed Graham to the rear of the garage, walking between the borrowed Citroen and the small delivery truck that I had noticed when we arrived the night before last. Along the back wall stood a row of tall cupboards. Graham opened a cupboard door and rummaged around inside. After a moment she removed what at first looked like a black life preserver. She handed it to Aurora. Then Graham removed another one from the cupboard and handed it to me.

They were bulletproof vests.

"Put them on under your boiler suits," Graham said.

I said, "Do we need these?"

"I couldn't say. But if you wait until you need them to put them on, it will be too late."

Aurora and I unzipped the boiler suits and pulled our arms out of the sleeves. We let the upper portion of the suits fall over our hips while we put the bulletproof vests on and fastened the Velcro strips that held them tight to our torsos. The vests were covered with a rubberized material that didn't seem at all strong enough to stop a bullet. I wondered how effective these vests were, and hoped that I would never find out.

Graham had removed a third vest from the cupboard and was putting it on. Prescott-Browne stood to one side, holding the flashlight. He wasn't wearing a boiler suit and he didn't appear to be interested in a vest. Wherever we were going, he wasn't going with us.

When Graham had her vest on and her boiler suit back in place she reached into the same cupboard and felt around. When her hand reappeared she was holding a pump-action shotgun. She reached in again and retrieved a box of shells.

The sight of the riot gun gave me pause.

"No need to get edgy," Graham said. "This is all very routine."

The delivery truck was parked nose-out. Prescott-Browne stepped over and pulled open the double doors of the cargo box and motioned for Aurora and I to climb in. We balked. What was the purpose of loading us into the cargo box? Graham tried to reassure us. We couldn't ride in the cab of the truck because once the sun came up we'd be visible to anyone on the road.

The inside of the cargo box was cramped and smelled of fertilizer. Steel shelves were bolted to the sides. There was a small window in the forward wall of the cargo box that lined up with the back window of the truck's cab. Aurora and I climbed in and hunched down and shuffled forward. The soles of our shoes scratched across the dirt-covered floor of the box. We crouched down next to the window and tried to get comfortable.

Prescott-Browne closed the doors.

It was going to be a long ride.

I heard the door of the truck cab open and close. I looked through the connecting windows and could just make out Graham as she pulled the seat belt across her and fastened it. I heard the overhead garage doors being pushed up and, a moment later, the sound of a car door slamming closed. The Citroen's engine sputtered to life. Prescott-Browne revved the cold engine several times. He seemed now to be making as much noise as possible. The Citroen's headlights came on just as Graham started up the delivery truck.

She let the engine idle quietly. She kept the truck's lights off.

Prescott-Browne revved the Citroen's engine some more.

Then he threw the transmission into reverse gear and backed out of the garage. He turned the car around on the gravel. He shifted gears and popped the clutch and the Citroen jumped forward and started down the tree-lined dirt path toward the main road. The buzz saw whine of the revved up engine straining against the low gear filled the darkness.

As the Citroen moved off I could make out Graham releasing the parking brake and pushing the truck's stick shift into gear. Without turning on the headlights Graham pulled the delivery truck out of the garage and onto the gravel. Instead of following the Citroen out to the main road, Graham turned the truck sharply to the left. She drove slowly along a dirt track that led out into a field behind the house and to the right of the greenhouses. We were heading in the opposite direction of the main road and I realized now what the plan was. Prescott-Browne's loud exit was supposed to draw attention away from our more surreptitious departure. In case the house was being watched from the road.

Prescott-Browne was a decoy.

Graham crept the truck forward at a slow and steady speed. The surface of the dirt track was uneven and Aurora and I were bounced and jostled inside the cargo box. For several minutes we heard tree branches brushing the side of the truck. Then the truck's tires landed on a smooth surface.

Graham hit the headlights.

We were on a proper road now. The truck gained speed.

We were on our way north, to Lyon.

Dawn broke an hour after we left the nursery. The sky looked gray and forbidding. The fields along the roadway looked bare. Just another chill morning in the south of France. Certainly not the kind of weather that one saw advertised in the travel brochures. Not that I gave much of a shit about travel brochures. I'd had quite enough of the south of France.

The ride was smooth once we reached the A7 highway.

"I don't know if I want to return to England," Aurora said, all of a sudden.

"It's a little late for that discussion," I said.

"Do you think Ali is still alive?"

"I don't honestly care."

"I do."

"I don't see why."

"Whatever else he is, he is a friend. Or was. He was always kind to me. He's not as barking mad as people think. It seems wrong just to leave him to be killed by the Rising Sun or the police or whomever."

"You've been ratting him out to MI6."

"I only told them little things."

"I'm not sure he'll see the distinction."

"If he's still alive, he must be in Algeria by now."

"Tough luck for Algeria."

The conversation died out. I wondered if Aurora and El-Kef had had a more intimate relationship than I'd gathered. I wasn't sure how I felt about that but I resolved not to mull it over. Right now our lives were in the hands of people I didn't fully trust, in the hope that they could save us from people who I didn't trust at all. Questions of who had slept with whom and why and the flotsam and jetsam of personal feelings didn't enter into the picture much, except as grim comedy.

I glanced now and then through the connecting windows at the road ahead. I had just noticed a road sign that indicated that Lyon was still 60 miles farther on when Graham slowed the truck down and guided it onto a highway exit ramp. I looked through the windows again. I saw a road sign that read VALENCE.

An arrow on the sign directed us to the town.

Did we need gasoline? Or a bathroom stop? No doubt such ordinary things happened during a well-orchestrated "exfiltration."

But rather than turning to the right, toward the town of Valence, Graham turned to the left at the first intersection. We passed under the highway and drove out into the countryside. If she wanted gasoline, she was driving in the wrong direction. And if it was a bathroom stop Graham wanted, she was planning on doing it rough.

After a few miles Graham turned off the country lane and onto a gravel road. Along either side of the road trellises of grape vines stretched in orderly rows for acres. A vineyard. The vines looked like bouquets of bare twigs. The dirt road curved around to the front of a two-story stucco villa painted in a fading pastel yellow.

Graham pulled the truck up to the front of the house and parked.

"What is this place?" Aurora said. Her cheek brushed against mine as we peered through the connecting windows at what lay outside. The truck shuddered as Graham turned off the engine. I had noticed as we approached the house that the rows of vineyard trellises rose on a gradual incline toward a flat hilltop in the distance.

Just then Graham opened the doors of the cargo box. We climbed out. The air smelled fresh on the cool wind but the smell of the fertilized cargo box lingered in my nostrils. I walked around in a circle to get the circulation back in my legs. Aurora opted for deep knee bends. Graham stood with her hands on her hips and studied the tall windows along the front of the two-story villa. She looked concerned.

"Are you expecting trouble?" I said.

Graham's eyes moved along the two rows of curtained windows, then came to rest on the northern corner of the building, where a dirt road led around the side of the house to the rear.

"It's not usually so silent here," Graham said.

I said, "Where's the airfield?"

"It's in Lyon."

"But we're not."

"How very observant of you, Mister Slade."

Without another word Graham walked off. She marched along the front of the house to the northern end. Aurora looked at me, as though waiting for me to explain. I could only shrug. Graham had driven us here for some purpose or another. Now she seemed puzzled. Whatever it was Graham had expected to find when she arrived wasn't here.

Aurora looked up at the sky. The wind was blowing storm clouds in from the west. In the distance I could see dark gray patches under the clouds where rain was already falling over the countryside. I walked out to the low rock wall that stood forty feet or so from the front of the villa.

Parked along the southern wall of the villa was a late model BMW sedan. Black, with tinted windows and a Paris license plate.

I walked down to the far corner of the house where Graham had disappeared. Graham now stood in the middle of a dirt road that led to a large white garage that stood fifty yards behind the house.

Graham's head scanned right to left, left to right. Surveying the landscape. When she turned around she still looked concerned. What did she hope to see, or not see? After a minute I walked back to the truck. I was worried. What were we doing here? What did Graham have up her sleeve? I kept my eyes on the tall windows at the front of the villa. Hoping to catch a glimpse of a curtain moving. A face appearing. A hand pushing a window open. But the curtains in the windows remained still.

After a minute Graham reappeared at the northern end of the villa. Her short legs seemed to work hard to keep her round torso moving forward as she approached us. In her white boiler suit she looked like an overfed duck with an appointment to keep.

She went to the truck and opened the driver's door and reached inside. She came out holding the riot gun. She pushed the door closed and paused and studied the front windows once more. She held the riot gun in both hands with the barrel pointed at the sky. Right out in plain sight.

She motioned for us to follow her.

"Let's have a look inside," Graham said.

I stood my ground, or thought I did. "I want to know why we're not going to Lyon."

Graham's eyebrows arched. A deep cleft formed above the bridge of her nose. Graham didn't like having to explain herself. She shifted the position of the riot gun. I noticed that the barrel of the riot gun was now pointed at a spot a few inches to the left of my right knee.

"This was always the plan," Graham said. "I was directed to bring you as far as this house. It is a safe house. We are here to meet a colleague. He will escort you the rest of the way to the airfield." Graham turned to look over her shoulder at the storm clouds moving in fast. "And, as a further comment, I would be very much surprised if you were flown anywhere today. That storm will be upon us shortly. It doesn't look like top-notch flying weather. You may be cooling your heels here for another day."

"So where is your colleague?"

Graham looked chagrined. I saw the weariness in her eyes. "Do give me some credit, Mister Slade. Your ignorance of the matter at hand is not a condition shared by the larger world."

I wasn't so sure.

We climbed the three steps at the front of the house. The wooden door was full of ancient gouges, as though someone had once tried to open it with an ice pick. Graham took hold of the solid iron door knocker. She raised it and then slammed it back down against the metal pad underneath, four times. Thick dull sounds arose from the door. No other sounds followed. I felt a raindrop on my face and then another as Graham applied the knocker to the door again. Still no response. She reached out for the iron door handle and pressed down on the latch and pushed.

The door swung open on dry hinges. Graham looked surprised.

She prodded the door open farther with the barrel of the riot gun. Then she stepped inside.

Aurora and I followed.

We stood in an entrance hallway. The hallway opened onto a main hall that was long and full of dust motes that floated in the light filtering in through the window curtains. A wide staircase on the left side of the room led up to the second floor. The room smelled of musty carpets and wasn't noticeably warmer than the outdoors.

Graham moved over to the wood-paneled wall and flipped a light switch. A soft light from clam-shelled wall sconces wafted down to the floor. It didn't help much. Graham moved farther into the room and called out the name of her colleague.

"Nightingale."

The name made me smile. Another code name. like *Bluebird*. But something was amiss.

"I thought we were meeting 'Bluebird,'" I said.

"He's in Lyon," Graham said. "Don't be impertinent."

Aurora folded her arms and gave me a worried look. The light filtering in through the curtained windows suddenly dimmed as Graham called out twice more for her colleague, Nightingale. In the silence that followed I heard a light tapping at the windows. It had begun to rain.

Aurora said, "Nightingale has flown the coop."

Graham repositioned the shotgun, then reached into the pocket of her boiler suit and removed a cell phone. Opened the cover. "Let's just give him a ring." The small electronic screen lit up in soft blue. It seemed like the brightest light in the room. Graham entered a phone number with her thumb. Held the phone up to her ear. After a moment she lowered it and hit the cancel button. Then she tapped the redial button on the phone. Again she frowned. Lowered the phone. Closed the lid.

"No service," Graham said.

"Is it charged?" Aurora said.

"Certainly."

"Perhaps the storm is interrupting service."

Graham shook her head. She looked distracted. "He was

supposed to have called me this morning, but he didn't. So I tried to call him. On the highway, just after we left Marseille. I could get no service then either. Odd." Graham slid the phone back in her pocket.

"There is the car outside," Aurora said.

"Are you sure the car belongs to him?" I said to Graham.

"It could only be his car."

But Graham didn't sound certain of that.

We proceeded into the room on the other side of the staircase. The room was empty except for two bookcases covered with white bed sheets. We examined the kitchen and a couple of back rooms on the first floor and then moved upstairs. The wooden stairs creaked and shifted under my feet. They were covered by a thick layer of dust. It didn't look to me like anyone had spent any time in this house in the last ten years.

The bedrooms upstairs were bare. Thin mattresses lay on the sagging springs of old bed frames. There were no pillows or sheets or blankets. No dressing tables or mirrors or armoires. In one room we were surprised to find a throw rug lying in the center of the floor. But Nightingale—whoever he was—wasn't hiding underneath. Outside the storm rolled in fast. Rain now pelted the windows. Gusts of wind rattled the window frames. Maybe Nightingale hadn't arrived. Maybe that wasn't his car parked outside. Maybe something had gone deeply wrong with Graham's plans. Or did Graham have another plan—one that she wasn't sharing with us? It was an uncomfortable thought. Graham had been right about one thing though. The storm was going to keep us from flying.

When would we get out of here? When could I stop looking over my shoulder, waiting for the sound of the other shoe dropping?

We saved the basement for last. And that was where we found Nightingale.

He was very much dead.

The other shoe had dropped.

23

The body lay on the concrete floor. On its side, with legs drawn up and arms bent at the elbows. A crusted trail of blood stretched from the corner of the corpse's mouth and down the cheek to the floor. A distended tongue covered the bottom row of the front teeth. There were two small holes in the fabric of Nightingale's sweater, right about the center of the chest. The weave of the sweater in the area around the holes was no longer bright blue, but black with dried blood.

He'd been dead for a while.

Nightingale's bow tie had been pulled violently to one side of his neck, trapping the collar of his shirt underneath. Like he'd been dragged across the floor by the tie. His eyes were wide open and staring into the shadows underneath a nearby work table. There were a few smears of dried blood on the concrete around the body, but not many. I wondered if he was killed elsewhere and then dumped here. Then I wondered what difference it made.

He was dead. That was all.

I looked at Graham. Her face was drained of color and her lips were pressed together hard. I could see her jaw muscles clench as she kneeled down and pressed two fingers to the side of the corpse's neck, looking for a pulse.

It was a hopeless effort, but Graham had to be sure.

Her fingers fell away. She stared into the lifeless face of her colleague. As though searching for last images frozen in the glassy pupils. She reached down again and this time her hand went into Nightingale's pants pocket. She felt around inside, then her hand reappeared.

Holding Nightingale's cell phone.

A low grunt came from the corner of Graham's mouth as she stood up and her old bones settled into new positions. She opened the dead man's phone. Tapped in a number and raised the phone to her ear. She frowned. She lowered the phone and disconnected the call and then redialed. The look that now came over Graham's face was hard.

"There is no service to Nightingale's phone either," Graham said. She closed the phone.

I said, "Is there a landline in the house?"

Graham gave me a thin smile. "There hasn't been a land line for many years, Mister Slade. This is the age of cellular electronics, or haven't you heard." The thin smile fell and became a look of disgust. "It would seem that progress has most decidedly thrown us into a ditch."

"We can't stay here," Aurora said. The words tumbled out quickly.

I agreed. A hasty exit was called for.

Graham ignored our acute concerns. She picked up the riot gun and tucked it under her arm. She paused over the corpse, then knelt down once more and fussed with the bow tie until it lay properly under the dead man's chin and the shirt collar was pressed back into place. It wasn't clear to me what the practical effect of this was. I was sure Nightingale no longer cared about his general tidiness. As an afterthought, Graham tried to poke the dead man's swollen bluish tongue back into his mouth with the tip of her finger. She didn't have much success.

Graham outlined a change of plan as Aurora and I followed her upstairs to the kitchen.

"Aurora, my dear, I would like you to take the truck and drive into Valence," Graham said. "I'm going to give you Brownie's cell phone number. Find a café or a gas station in Valence with a public telephone. Call him and let him know that we have reached Station Twelve but that things have gone a bit pear-shaped. We need some assistance in reorienting Mister Nightingale. 'Reorienting'—Brownie will understand. He'll need some time to look into things, so give him the number of the phone you call him from and then have a cup of tea and wait for him to call back. Once he has, return here and we'll proceed on the basis of whatever instructions he gives you. Mister Slade and I will stay here and sweep up."

Graham spoke with no more emotion in her voice than if she had been outlining the seating arrangements for a hand of canasta. I found her coolness a little unsettling. What possible reason could there be for us to stay here? It seemed obvious to me that we needed to leave, immediately, all three of us, and I said so again.

Graham disagreed.

"It won't do," she said. "We can't leave Nightingale behind. I don't leave my dead on the field of battle. But equally, we can't toss him into the truck and trundle him off until we have a suitable place to deposit him. And then, of course, there is the problem of how to get you both to London as expeditiously as possible. In light of the weather conditions, the flight from Lyon is most definitely out of the running for the time being. In sum, there is no point in scampering off helter-skelter until we know where exactly we are scampering to."

"Nightingale was shot," I said. "Which means that someone was here to do the shooting. That someone might still be in the neighborhood."

We were crossing the main hall now. Graham patted the barrel of the riot gun. "And that would be quite all right. We are not without resources. Don't you have any backbone, Mister Slade?"

"I have one. It's a good one. And I'd like it to stay right where it is. Rather than have it blown into small pieces by large caliber firearms."

We reached the front door and Graham pulled it open. Sheets of rain blew inside on gusts of wind. The sky was darker now and the weather had grown even more foul. It was hard to believe that it was nine o'clock in the morning. It looked like night had fallen.

Graham handed me the riot gun. "Try not to injure yourself with that," she said.

Then she slipped outside into the storm.

Graham raced to the cab of the truck on the toes of her boots, bird-like, as though she had just stepped out of the bathtub and was scurrying to the towel rack. It was a mannerism that looked extremely odd in a portly and heavily-booted woman of seventy years. She reached the truck and pulled open the passenger-side door and climbed in. Slammed the door shut. Turned the overhead cab light on. Her outline was diffuse behind the rain-covered truck windows as she moved around inside the cab. Then the cab light went out and the driver's door flew open. Graham climbed out and rushed back toward the house in her curious avian way.

When she was back inside and I had the front door closed she reached into the oversized waist pocket of her boiler suit and pulled out a large revolver. Chrome-plated and snub-nosed.

"It's a spare," she said. She handed the revolver to me. "It might make you feel better about things."

I handed the shotgun back to her and took the revolver. I hefted it in my hand. It was a Smith & Wesson model—the name was stamped on the butt. I felt an urge to do something coolly professional, like slapping the cylinder out to inspect the cartridges. I fumbled with the release, then turned the pistol every which way trying to slide the cylinder open. The five rounds loaded into the cylinder nearly fell out. Then I smashed the tip of my finger slapping the cylinder back into place. Somehow I succeeded in getting the empty chamber in the cylinder lined up with the hammer, and the revolver tucked back into my pocket, without shooting myself.

Graham turned to Aurora. "The keys are in the ignition. I wrote Brownie's phone number on a business card that I left on the gearshift console. Drive down to the main road and then follow the signs to Valence. You do drive, don't you, dear?"

"I can drive."

"Very well then."

Aurora looked at me uncertainly. I took hold of her hand in both of mine. "Be careful," I said.

It was an unnecessary remark, under the circumstances.

I opened the front door. Aurora, head down against the wind and rain, slipped out into the storm. She climbed into the truck and started the engine and turned on the headlights. She pulled the truck forward and turned it around on the gravel and slowly drove off down the access road that led out to the main road. In a moment all I could see through the driving rain was the barest outline of the back of the truck and the glow of the red taillights.

Then even the taillights disappeared into the storm.

I closed the door.

Graham had gone into the kitchen. I joined her there and watched as she searched the kitchen drawers until she found what she wanted—a paring knife. The steel blade was four inches long.

We went back downstairs. Nightingale was right where we had left him, no surprise there. Graham handed me the knife and leaned the shotgun against a stack of cardboard boxes. She went to a cupboard on the other side of the basement and inspected the contents. She didn't find what she was looking for there, but in a wooden fruit crate on a shelf underneath a termite-eaten workbench she found a loose bundle of what looked like clothesline cord.

Graham brought the cord over and handed it to me. "We've got to tie up Nightingale, good and proper. We can't have his appendages flopping about as we transport him over hill and dale."

Graham told me to cut off a section of cord, about a meter and a half in length. Then untangle the rest of it. I cut the requested length of cord and handed it to her. I dropped the knife into the chest pocket of my boiler suit and untangled the rest of the cord. For her part, Graham knelt beside the corpse and searched the clothes. She found Nightingale's wallet and key ring and the electronic key to his car. She placed the items in her own pockets.

Does he have a gun?" I said.

Graham shook her head. "He never carried one. He was not a violent person."

Graham got to her feet again. She studied the basement clutter that surrounded us. The cast-off furniture, the cardboard boxes, an empty rain barrel. She walked over and poked around in the junk stacked near an ancient washing machine. She found a plastic basket filled with what looked like bed sheets and towels. She pulled a wadded yellowing sheet from off the top of the pile.

At her direction we folded the sheet in half lengthwise and then in half again, so that we had a long and relatively narrow length of cloth. We laid the sheet on the floor a few feet from the corpse. Then we picked up the corpse by the feet and under the shoulders and lifted it onto the sheet and straightened the arms and legs. Finally we brought the sheet up and over and tucked it under the other side of the corpse so that the sheet covered it entirely.

"What was his real name?" I said.

Graham was a little out of breath. "His real name?"

"The name he used when he wasn't using a code name."

"'Nightingale' was his real name."

"You don't say."

"His code name was 'Smith'."

I lifted the corpse's legs a few inches off the floor, wrapped the shorter length of cord around the ankles, and then tied it off. Graham lifted the head and torso of the corpse enough so that I could tie the longer length of cord around the arms and midriff. When we were done we stood over the tightly-wrapped package and inspected our work.

Graham said, "Nightingale had some eccentric pastimes, but I don't believe being tied up like an old carpet was one of them." Graham paused, in thought. Then, "But I could be mistaken about that."

24

Upstairs in the kitchen Graham tried to use her cell phone again. Then she tried Nightingale's phone once more. Neither of them could be made to work. No signal. The phones were dead to the world. Just like Nightingale. Meanwhile the wind rattled the windows and the rain fell in black sheets. Lightening flashed. Thunder rumbled. The weather had suddenly become orchestrated.

"It's because of the storm," I said.

Graham was silent.

I said, "Either that, or both the phones are broken."

Graham slipped the phones into her pocket. Finally she said, "As I think I've mentioned, the first time I tried to ring Nightingale was shortly after we departed the nursery. I could get no signal even then. I assumed that it was a problem with my phone, or with Nightingale's. The storm, of course, was nowhere near us. Nor had it arrived here."

Graham looked away. She crossed the kitchen. She took hold of the edge of the sink counter and raised herself up on the tips of her boots so that she could peer out of the window above the sink. She looked in the direction of the garage that stood behind and a little to the north of the house. I couldn't imagine that she could see much of it, the weather being what it was.

I said, "It's quite a storm."

"It certainly is."

"It wouldn't be odd if it disrupted the phone service."

"No, not terribly odd."

But something was eating at Graham. She wanted to go outside. Take a look inside the garage that stood behind the house. I couldn't imagine why. Our course of action seemed clear to me. Wait for Aurora to return. Then implement Prescott-Browne's plan, whatever it might be, and get the hell out of here.

I said, "What do you think is out there?"

"Maybe nothing at all."

"But you don't believe that."

Graham raised her hand and scratched her knobby chin as she thought out loud. "I don't know what to believe. But I am certainly aware that there are numerous types of apparatus that will block a signal from a mobile phone. Police agencies use them quite regularly. They help to keep the riff-raff at bay while the police descend in force."

"You think one is being used against us, right now."

Graham took a deep breath. "I don't necessarily think anything. I'm merely considering the possibilities. But if we want to add to the sum of our knowledge, we must explore. Need I remind you, Mister Slade, I am in the intelligence business. I am not in the ignorance business."

Graham wanted me to go outside with her. Or maybe she wanted me to go in her place. Either way she was going to be disappointed. I wasn't leaving the house. I wasn't going anywhere until Aurora returned. We'd been all over this house. The one thing I knew for certain was that there was no one in this house with us. Except for Nightingale. But he was no threat, as near as I could tell.

Graham had other ideas.

"Let us review," she said. "Nightingale was killed. Not in the last hour or two, but assuredly not so very long ago. Which means that someone was here to kill him, as you yourself so cleverly pointed out. Now, why would anyone want to kill Nightingale before we met up with him? One obvious answer presents itself. He was killed to keep from warning us that we were entering a trap and would be captured or killed ourselves. He was murdered to keep him from sounding the alarm. But that leaves us with a further question. Why go to the bother of setting a trap if you are not going to stay behind to spring it."

I looked around the kitchen. I raised my open hands in a dumb show gesture and shrugged theatrically. Like a circus clown who can't discover how the flower squirts water.

"Where would the trap be?" I said.

"That is one question."

Right then a flash of lightning lit up the kitchen. Followed closely by thunder that seemed to reverberate through the house. It was even more theatrical than my sarcastic clown look.

I realized that my mind was wandering. I was more tired than I thought. I needed to stay focused. I was armed and standing in a kitchen with an elderly Englishwoman who was also armed, and there was a murdered man tied up in the basement. I didn't need to go looking for the absurd. The absurd was right here with us. We were living it. And it wasn't so comical.

Graham went on. "If we assume that Nightingale was killed to keep him from raising an alarm, then we must also conclude that the trap was to be sprung right here," she said. "As we know, there is no one here in the house with us, except for poor Nightingale. The only other place for someone to hole up and wait to spring their trap would be the garage outside. And so, it is outside to the garage that we must go."

"I'm not going with you."

"The first rule of making a good defensive position is to secure your perimeter. And we are, right now, very much on the defense. We've searched the house itself. Now a reconnoitering of the garage is indicated. Whether you want to go or not."

"I don't."

"We must preserve a margin of safety."

"You preserve it."

Graham scowled. "You're not much good in a pinch, are you."

"I'm not going out there, that's all. I'll wait here. In case someone calls."

I smiled at the joke. Graham didn't. Her eyes looked as grim as the outdoors. She gave up on me and returned to the kitchen window. She studied the storm some more, then disappeared downstairs. When she returned ten minutes later she was carrying a small sheet of blue plastic tarp. The kind of tarp that a painter might use as a drop cloth.

"As good a raincoat as any," she said. "Give me your revolver, Mister Slade. It will be easier to travel with in this weather than a shotgun. "

We traded weapons. She took the revolver and with a

quick pull and a flick of her wrist she opened the cylinder and inspected the cartridges, then spun the cylinder and slapped it back in place. It was the cool and professional maneuver that I had wanted to perform earlier, but couldn't. I felt a pang of guilt for letting her go outside alone. Still, I saw no reason to accompany her. Aurora would return soon and then we'd leave, all of us together.

Graham gave me a scornful look and tucked the revolver into her boiler suit. She folded the square of plastic tarp over once. Then she cut a slit in it with a kitchen knife and pulled the plastic over her head and let it fall over her shoulders and around her body.

Graham opened the kitchen door. A rush of cold wind and rain blew in. The door opened onto a long covered porch and she crossed the porch and descended the porch stairs. I followed her out as far as the steps. Maybe just to show her that I wasn't entirely unmindful of the situation.

I stood on the porch and watched her as she started off along the flagstone path that paralleled the stone wall between the house and the edge of the vineyard. The garage stood to the northeast. From the porch I could just make out the garage's roof. A single light burned over the sliding doors. It hadn't been on earlier. No doubt it operated on a photoelectric cell that had caused it to come on when the storm rolled in. I watched Graham's bundled blue figure as she moved along the stone path. She reached the end of the path and slipped out of sight behind the vineyard trellises and the darkness of the storm.

I stepped back inside and closed the door.

Graham was plain wrong. We needed to get out of here. This wasn't a time for reconnoitering and digging in. This was a time for fleeing, and Nightingale's earthly remains be damned. I thought of Aurora again. I wondered if she was sitting in a warm café right now. Waiting for Prescott-Browne to call back. Drinking a hot cup of coffee. I could've gone for a hot cup of coffee right then. More than anything. I looked around the kitchen. Started searching though the cupboards and drawers. Taking stock. I found a battered coffee percolator in one of the cupboards. I found porcelain tea cups covered with a flowery pattern in another cupboard. But there was no coffee. No tea. No cocoa. No broth. Nightingale hadn't laid in any provisions. I turned on the taps in the kitchen sink and got a few drips of rust-colored water, then nothing. I stood at the sink and watched the storm rage outside. I heard the sharp crack of thunder.

A second later I paused. The thunder hadn't sounded right.

Then I heard it again.

I was sure now. It wasn't thunder. It sounded too sharp. Too small. Too close.

It sounded like a gunshot.

I grabbed the riot gun and rushed outside. The hard winds seemed to push the torrents of rain sideways and the roof over the porch offered little protection. I moved down to the end of the porch where a wide column held up one corner of the porch roof. I stood against the south side of the column and peered around it to the north. Toward the end of the flagstone path, and the garage farther on.

The soft electric light burned over the garage doors. The rain lashed at me. I waited to hear another gunshot but all I heard was the wind howling in my ears. I squinted my eyes against the rain that pelted my face.

I waited. The thunder and lightning pressed down on the

landscape like a dead weight. Soon I was soaked to the skin. I decided I was wrong about the gunshot. It was the thunder after all. My nerves were getting the best of me. Making me hear things. Graham was right, I wasn't cut out for his kind of work. Not much good in this kind of pinch. But there was no shame in that, that I could see. To hell with Graham. I decided to return to the kitchen. I'd had enough of this game of cowboys and Indians.

Then I noticed something moving out in the storm. Coming around the edge of the vineyard. From the direction of the garage.

It wasn't Graham.

It was the figure of a man, I was sure.

The man wore a hooded green rain poncho. He walked along the flagstone path toward the porch. The rain poncho hung to his knees. The hood was pulled over his head. He walked slowly, his head bent to keep his eyes on the ground before him. Careful to keep to the stone path and avoid the mud holes. His arms were tucked under the poncho. The bottom edges of the poncho whirled around his legs in the wind. His face was nothing but a dark oval hidden inside the deep poncho hood.

I ducked behind the porch column. I didn't think he'd seen me. I raised the riot gun parallel to my body to keep it hidden behind the column. It occurred to me now that I'd never fired the shotgun. It was a pump action model. Was there a shell in the chamber or did I need to pump one in?

The man was only a few yards away from me now, coming up on my left side. The ground was three feet lower than the porch and the man's eyes were on the path before him and I hoped he wouldn't notice me as he passed the column.

No doubt the poncho hood blocked his peripheral vision. I held the shotgun in both hands now. One hand forward on the buttstock, just behind the trigger, and one hand on the pump lever.

I waited.

The man walked past the column. He didn't turn his head.

I let him take another step. Then I pulled back hard and worked the pump lever to draw a shell into the shotgun's chamber, at the same time lowering the barrel so that it was pointed at the figure in the poncho.

I took one step forward. I braced my legs and steadied the gun. I hoped that I looked mean as hell.

The man in the poncho stopped. After a long motionless pause he turned slowly. He must've recognized the sound. There are few things as distinctive as the sound of a shell being rammed into the chamber of a riot gun. It doesn't sound like anything else. No way to mistake it.

The man on the flagstone path raised his head now. I felt hail grazing my cheek. I still couldn't see his face. The poncho hood was large and it hid his features well. The barrel of the riot gun was pointed at his chest, dead center. If I fired now there was no chance that I'd miss.

The man said, "Richard, you're not going to shoot me."

I recognized the voice immediately.

It belonged to Septimus Morgan.

25

We stood in the kitchen. Morgan stood at one end of the counter and I stood at the other. Morgan had taken off the rain poncho and it lay on the floor in a wet heap. He'd also set down the automatic pistol that he'd carried under the poncho. He pushed it down the kitchen counter toward me and told me that I was lucky. He could've easily shot me. The gun under the poncho had been pointed at me.

I hadn't seen him in two years. He looked older than he should have. His eyes were dark and clouded, as though the rough weather outside had caught in his eyes and taken root. The brown hair was spotted with gray and the jaw line that had once been square was now receding under loose skin. His hands looked callused and knotty and I noticed that his knuckles were scraped raw. His bulky green sweater hung off him like a carpet of moss.

The smile on his face seemed more crooked than it once was.

"Morgan, I know who you are," I said. Not knowing where else to begin. "And I know you just shot Graham."

"I didn't come here to shoot you," he said. "If that's what

191

you think."

"Is she dead?"

"That would be my guess." The crooked smile faded. Morgan folded his arms across his chest. He leaned back against the counter and gave me an appraising look. "Would you feel better if Graham had shot me and I was lying out there in the mud right now? She wasn't your friend, Richard. She intended to have you killed."

"Maybe you do too. Did you kill Nightingale?"

"Who?"

"The man downstairs. The dead one."

"Actually, his name was Smith."

"That was his code name."

"I'll be damned."

"What I can't figure out is why you killed him."

Morgan shook his head. "Richard, before we start shouting and pointing, let's get a few things out into the open. You said you know about me. What exactly do you think you know?"

I didn't answer at first. I picked up Morgan's pistol and slipped it into my pocket. Then I stepped back from the counter, holding the riot gun in both hands. I stepped back farther until I reached the wall. Morgan was ten feet from me now. If it came to it, I could easily turn the shotgun on him and give him a belly full before he got too close. But would I do it? I wasn't sure. Graham was dead. I didn't know what to think about that. Mostly I felt numb.

I leaned against the wall and began. Reciting all of the things that I knew or that Graham had told me. How Morgan's life as a journalist was a cover story. He worked for the CIA. A dirty tricks outfit with a European brief. A judicious frown appeared on Morgan's face when I suggested that he might be an assassin. It was replaced by an apologetic look when I mentioned the note left at my hotel. The wind rattling the windows punctuated my claims and accusations. The crack of thunder filled my pauses. A look of deep concern spread across Morgan's face. I waited for him to launch into a litany of excuses, to discount in the strongest terms possible everything I had just said. But that wasn't what concerned him.

"Are you wearing a protective vest?" he said.

"What difference does it make."

"Graham gave it to you." It was a statement, not a question. Morgan unfolded his arms and stood up straight. He looked suddenly alert and wary. As though he suspected me of pulling one of his own dirty tricks on him.

He said, "Have you been keeping up with the news much, Richard?"

"I've been a little preoccupied."

"Maybe you've heard about this in your travels. The day before you arrived in France a man blew himself up inside the offices of an engineering firm in Lille. The firm is a front for French intelligence operations in North Africa and the Middle East, but that's neither here nor there. The man who blew himself up was a common sneak thief who was recruited to steal certain industrial secrets. But the police caught wind of the break in, and when they arrived and attempted to capture him the bulletproof vest he was wearing exploded. He killed himself and took three policemen with him.

"The National Police later found documents in the man's apartment that linked him to the Rising Sun. But the documents were planted there. In reality, he was working for the British. It was another pathetic attempt by the British to

193

force the French to recognize that the Rising Sun is operating on French soil by staging an 'incident.' Unless I am sorely mistaken, it was the British who gave that man the vest and advised him to wear it. And it was also the British who detonated it by remote control.

"Does any of this ring a bell, Richard?"

"That can't be true," I said. My voice was a dull croak. My throat had gone dry. The bulletproof vest that covered my torso suddenly felt like the jaws of a vise.

Morgan went on. "Richard, we've had Smith under surveillance for months. We've had him covered with so many bugs that he couldn't scratch himself without us hearing him. We knew that Graham was bringing you here. And that you'd be handed off to Smith. We also know that Smith wasn't planning on taking you to a plane. He was going to hide you and the girl in a safe house in Lyon. And I'd be willing to bet that at some point the police in Lyon would have gotten an anonymous tip concerning your whereabouts. Maybe from Smith, maybe from someone else. When they turned up to capture you, you and the girl and the police would have been blown to smithereens. A replay of the Lille incident. And since you've already been tied to the Rising Sun, it would be one more pointed stick that MI6 could use to push the French in the right direction."

Morgan cocked his head to one side. "By the way, where is the girl?"

"She drove into town."

"She's coming back?"

"She went to call one of Graham's colleagues in Marseille. To get instructions on how to proceed. Now that Nightingale is dead."

"She's wearing a vest also?"

I said that she was.

Morgan shook his head. "You'd better hope she doesn't get into a car accident or fall down a flight of stairs. *Plastique* is a relatively stable explosive but that's no guarantee. It's only as safe as the detonator it's attached to. Take off that vest, Richard. Do it slowly. Let's get it out of the house."

"Graham wore a vest. She didn't explode, did she? When you shot her."

"That doesn't mean that your vest is safe."

Could I believe anything Morgan said? I decided that I couldn't. All the same, it wouldn't cost me anything to get rid of the vest.

I set the shotgun down on the kitchen table, close enough to me that I could grab it fast if need be. I kept my eyes on Morgan as I unzipped the front of the boiler suit and pulled my arms from the arms of the suit. The top portion of the boiler suit hung around my waist. The black vest was completely exposed. Morgan motioned for me to stop moving. He stepped forward. I took a step back and told him to stay where he was. He told me to calm down. He told me to pull out his pistol and point it at him if I felt in danger. I let it go. I was sure I could wrestle him to the ground, if it came to that.

Morgan reached out and inspected the Velcro straps that were fastened at my sides. Then he ran his hand lightly along the front of the vest. Feeling for something. High on the left side his hand stopped moving.

Morgan's finger lightly traced an oval shape just under the surface of the vest. "That's the detonator," he said. "Embedded in the vest. It should be reasonably safe, unless you start

195

pounding on it with a hammer. Of course, some detonators are better than others. It's best to assume the worst."

"What sets the detonator off, normally?"

"An electronic signal."

"Say, from a cell phone?"

"It's possible."

Morgan retreated back to the counter. He made a lifting motion with his hands. "Unfasten the vest and pull it off. Slowly. There's no rush. I'm fairly sure that the one person who could have detonated it with a remote is dead. Pull it off and hang on to it. Don't drop it on the floor."

I felt beads of sweat forming on my forehead. When I had the first strap unfastened I felt an irrational urge to tear the vest off any which way. I swallowed hard. I told myself to be calm. As Morgan had said, there was no rush. *Plastique is a relatively stable explosive.* Morgan watched me closely. *But that's no guarantee.* I got the three straps on the right side unfastened and went to work on the three to my left. As I unfastened the first strap on the left side Morgan sneezed. I nearly jumped out of my skin.

"Steady, Richard."

But I wasn't steady. My hands shook as I unfastened the second strap. There was one strap left. I took a deep breath. Morgan stared at my hands as I unfastened the last strap. Nothing happened. The nylon ends of the strap fell down along my side but that was all.

I tucked my thumbs under the vest and lifted it off my shoulders.

"Let's take it outside," Morgan said.

Morgan stepped over to the back door and opened it.

The wind and the rain crossed the porch and entered the

kitchen like an angry guest. We walked out onto the covered porch. Stepped down off the porch and onto the flagstone path. The rain fell hard and stung my face. The sky was black. I held the vest at arm's length as I followed Morgan. We moved along the path towards the southern end of the house. The opposite direction from the garage. I wondered what would happen if the vest slipped out of my hands. Would that be enough to detonate it? I couldn't see how. I'd been wearing the vest all morning. Aurora and I had been bounced around in the back of the truck all the way from Marseille and the vest hadn't done a thing.

We reached the corner of the house. To my right was Nightingale's BMW sedan. Forty or so feet beyond the car was the stone well that I had noticed when we first arrived. The rain battered us. Morgan stopped and turned. He shouted at me and pointed at the well. He was only a few feet away but I couldn't hear him. The roar of the storm filled my ears.

But I understood.

The stone path ended. I was walking in mud now. A gust of wind tried to pull the vest out of my hands as I approached the well. My foot slipped and I lost my balance. I started to fall. I landed on one knee. Still holding the vest at arm's length. I took a deep breath and got back up onto my feet. I took another step and pressed my foot down hard into the mud. To make sure I had solid footing.

I was still ten feet from the well when my rising fear got the better of me.

I threw the vest. I hurled it toward the well. It landed on the stone lip of the well and for a second it lay there, motionless. I stared at it. Morgan stared at it. The front section of the vest was folded under the back. Half of it hung down into the well, while the other half seemed to have caught on one of the iron posts that had once held the crossbar for a water pail.

As we watched, the wind hit the vest and pushed it over the side. It fell into the darkness of the well.

I half expected an explosion, but none came.

We returned to the house without any further drama. We stood in the kitchen and dripped rainwater onto the floor. Morgan suggested that we go into the main hall and start a fire in the fireplace. No sense in catching a cold. His concern for my health seemed ill-placed. He gave me a curious look when I picked up the shotgun. Perhaps he was right about the vest and perhaps not, but I saw no reason why I should trust him.

I followed him into the main hall.

Morgan said, offhand, "Kind of funny when you think about it—a bulletproof vest that kills you more effectively than the bullet it saves you from. What will they think of next? You have to see the humor in things, Richard."

"Why did you kill Nightingale?"

Morgan reached the brick fireplace. A pile of short logs rested in a metal box that was pushed up against the bricks. Inside a smaller metal box were tinder sticks and yellowed pages of newspaper. Morgan didn't answer me. He pulled the fireplace screen aside. Bent down on one knee and wadded up some of the newspaper and tamped it down onto the iron grate. Placed two handfuls of tinder sticks onto the newspaper. Then he covered the newspaper and the sticks with four logs, positioning them with care.

He put a match to the newspaper. Soon the tinder sticks were burning. Small flames licked at the underside of the logs.

Morgan stared into the growing fire. Now he fielded my question as though I'd just asked it. "It's all part of the game, Richard. The Central Directorate broke through Graham's computer firewalls months ago. Yesterday a police tech unit in Paris intercepted e-mail traffic between Graham and Smith—or Nightingale, as you prefer. It said more or less that Graham would be escorting two individuals to this location, and that Smith would escort them the rest of the way to Lyon. The two individuals were referred to in the message traffic only as 'Jiggery' and 'Pokery.' I'm not sure which one you were, but it hardly matters. We knew from French surveillance that you had been spotted at a pub in Marseille that is a known way station for British intelligence assets. In the company of a man who was identified as Graham's factotum."

"Who spotted us in Marseille?"

Morgan picked up the fireplace poker and fussed with the logs. "Plainclothes French police. They were tipped off by the taxi driver who drove you in from Deux Pistoles. He wanted a reward. They gave him a kick in the ass and told him to get lost."

I thought of the two men at The Bourgeois Pig the night before last. Aurora had thought they might be El-Kef's men, or members of the Rising Sun. But no, they were French policemen. A hundred questions spun around in my head. So many that I couldn't sort them all out. I tried to come to terms with the idea that Morgan was working with the French security services. It wasn't easy.

Morgan went on. "The two flics were told to keep an eye on you but to wait for reinforcements before they grabbed you. Unfortunately, you disappeared before the cavalry got there."

"We went out the back door."

"The flics were chased out the front. By a gang of drunken Englishmen. Is there any other kind?" Morgan smiled to himself. He poked and prodded the fire some more. "So we focused on Graham. I arrived here last night to case the place and prepare a net in which to trap Graham and Smith. Mostly just microphones hidden around the house. And a jamming unit that blocks cell phone signals that I set up in the garage. Unfortunately, Smith turned up last night rather than this morning, when I expected him. He discovered me in the basement and, well, steps had to be taken."

Steps had to be taken. I thought of Nightingale's corpse wrapped in an ersatz funeral sheet. And Graham lying dead or dying outside in the mud. And here before me was Septimus Morgan. An old friend. A college buddy. I'd known him for twenty-five years but I realized now that I hadn't known him at all. He was a killer.

"Morgan, do you intend to kill me too?"

"Stop asking me that." Morgan set the poker aside. He stood up. The flames in the fireplace seemed to be reflected in his eyes. "Richard, you don't understand. Graham has used you from the start."

"It wasn't Graham who left a message at my hotel in Nice," I said. "It was you. If it hadn't been for that message, I wouldn't be here now."

"Why did you come to Nice at all?"

"I've been working on some poems. I thought you might help me get them published. I still had the idea that you were some kind of writer. That was my mistake."

Morgan stared at me. "You came here to show me poems?"

Morgan looked like he expected me to say something more.

Like he was waiting for a punch line. There wasn't one. He began to laugh anyway. It was a strong heartfelt laugh that seemed to travel up from deep inside of him. The laughter grew and he folded his arms across his chest and bent his head and laughed some more. I didn't think laughter was called for. Two people had died today and that was no laughing matter. But Morgan went on laughing. When the laughter finally died out he wiped a tear from his eye.

"The world doesn't need poems," Morgan said when he had composed himself. "What the world needs is guns. Guns and men who can use them. We are the good guys, Richard. In case you haven't heard. When I left that message at your hotel, I needed your help. Your country needed your help."

"It's got a funny way of asking."

Morgan the paid assassin—I wondered how long he'd been living this secret life. But what did it matter? The one thing that mattered was that a man that I had counted as a close friend had set me up. Framed me with a murder. Then let me run all over the south of France with the hounds of hell on my trail.

Smoke from the fireplace floated out into the room. Morgan turned and studied the stone face of the fireplace. He found the flue knob and turned it one way and then another. After a moment the smoke seemed to clear.

"Let me explain this to you," Morgan said now. The causal tone in his voice was gone. "Then you'll see things clearly. Without the smoke and mirrors. The Rising Sun is a terrorist organization—no two ways about it. But they are not fighting for an ideal. They are mercenaries, of the worst kind. They've been active here in France for many years now, working quietly. I've been assisting the Central

Directorate in keeping these people under surveillance. We've put together a small team—a dozen Frenchmen, mostly from the National Police, and myself. Outside of the men on the team, only a handful of French cabinet ministers and the CIA director himself know the full extent of the operation. My principal function is to liaise between the resources of the Agency and the team.

"But keeping tabs on the Rising Sun is dirty work. And when one is engaged in dirty work, one gets dirty.

"The British have also taken an interest in the Rising Sun. They seem to believe that the French aren't doing enough to fight them. So they've taken it upon themselves to convince the French that MI6 assistance is needed in France. The British would much rather fight the Rising Sun on foreign soil than on their own.

"When MI6 became aware that a Rising Sun asset was planning to take possession of some information stolen from the British Ministry of Defense, MI6 decided to set up a trap to expose the Rising Sun. The British would intercept the woman selling the information and replace her with a ringer. And to help them do that, they hired Ali El-Kef. Their goal was to create a situation that they could then feed to the French press. To show conclusively that the Rising Sun was a threat to the security of France, and that MI6 had the goods on them. But myself and my French colleagues decided to turn the tables on them. In order to get the British out from underfoot, so to speak.

"Before we could do that, a small wrinkle appeared. The Rising Sun asset who was to receive the stolen information had a heart attack in Nice. The day before you arrived. The Rising Sun sent a replacement, who we identified, and who

202

we detained in order to learn of any changes to the Rising Sun's plans. Of course, once we detained the second man we couldn't very well send him back out to complete his work. The problem of what to do with him was decided by the man himself, when he made a sloppy attempt to escape and caught a bullet for his trouble.

"So, as you can see, we needed someone to stand in for the second man. Someone who was obviously an outsider. Someone who was not connected in any way with the French police or the Central Directorate or the CIA. It was important to make people believe that you were who we said you were. A Rising Sun asset who was caught in the act."

I tried to take this all in. I said, "How did you find out the details of the drop?"

"Partly through our own intelligence assets. And partly from El-Kef."

"He works for you?"

"Through channels. El-Kef works for whoever pays him."

"The British thought he was working for them."

"He was."

"Who else is he working for?"

"Who knows. Who cares. He did what we told him to. And he did it without tipping us off to the British."

"They knew about you."

"They knew that I was in-country. They didn't know why. At least not until the deal went down. Then they pieced it together, but it was too late. We already had them by the short hairs."

"But your plan went haywire."

Morgan sighed. Raised his eyebrows. Looked down. He seemed to be studying the pattern in the rug that lay in front

203

of the sofa. "I don't know what happened there," he said. "The gunmen in Nice who ambushed you have been tied to El-Kef. So the National Police decided to round up the whole El-Kef operation in Sète—I understand that you were there too. Most unfortunate. What was also unfortunate was that El-Kef and most of his men escaped. But my unit has since uncovered other information. We now believe that the Rising Sun itself caught wind of our ruse and decided to step in. It's possible that they didn't know their second man had disappeared, and they believed that the man captured by the police was their man. So they decided to neutralize him before he could talk. And since some of the men involved in the ambush have been tied to El-Kef, then El-Kef must've been working with the Rising Sun as well."

There was a long silence while I tried to sort out Morgan's tale in my head. The British wanted to stage a ruse to convince the French that they needed British help in bringing the Rising Sun to justice. But Morgan's people were already working with the French, and they decided to stage their own ruse in order to expose the British gambit and get them out of the way for good. In the meantime, El-Kef decided to play all the ends against the middle and presumably contacted the Rising Sun to sell them the very secrets that the British had hired him to protect. Except that there were no secrets, as Graham had said. But the Rising Sun, unaware of that and also unaware that their second man was picked up by Morgan's team, thought I was he and tried to get rid of me in Nice, with the help of El-Kef's operation. Later, the Rising Sun might've gotten the idea that El-Kef had somehow double-crossed them, and they sent the man named Ivashko to settle accounts. But Ivashko was captured by El-Kef's men at Cannes and ended his days gulping sea water in a rusty cage.

"It was a ruse within a ruse within a ruse," I said. "And I got caught in the middle of it. Because I turned up in Nice looking for you."

Morgan scratched his head as he thought about it. The complexities and machinations. The lies and the intrigues. The smoke and the mirrors. He couldn't quite agree with my assessment. "It's not as bad as it sounds. You're not in any real danger, Richard. Now that I've found you."

"The Rising Sun wants to kill me."

"We'll take care of that end of it."

"How?"

Before Morgan could answer we heard a new sound from outside. We heard it over the howl of the wind and the pelting of the rain on the window panes. It sounded like a car engine.

Aurora.

Morgan crossed the room. He pulled the edge of a curtain aside and peered out the window. After a moment he let go of the curtain and turned and looked at me with no expression on his face.

A dead pan.

"My colleagues are here," Morgan said. "They'll be taking you to Paris. From there you'll fly home. Richard, right now I need you to put that shotgun down. Just lay it on the sofa. My colleagues might be jumpy. Seeing you standing there with a shotgun—they might get the idea you're going to use it. They're well-armed. Don't think for a second that they're not."

I looked down at the shotgun in my hands. I had a sick feeling in my stomach. It started to rise up to my throat.

I laid the shotgun down on the sofa and took a few steps to one side. I felt the heat from the fireplace on my back. Morgan hadn't adjusted the flue correctly and smoke from the fireplace was again collecting in the room. I watch Morgan cross the room and disappear into the foyer. I heard the front door open. The sounds of the storm tumbled in. The draft from outside blew the smoke from the fireplace into swirling patterns above my head.

I heard feet stamping on the floor. Then Morgan reappeared, with two men walking behind him. The men wore long dark overcoats with the collars turned up.

Morgan and one of the two men stepped into the main hall. The other man took up a position in the shadows at the edge of the foyer.

Flickers of light from the fireplace played over the faces of Morgan and the first man as they stepped into the center of the room.

The first man smiled.

It was Brissac. The police inspector who had interrogated me in Nice. The one from the National Police. I felt a sudden dizziness. An unsteadiness in my head and in my legs. The last few days were suddenly folding back on themselves. I was right back where I'd started. With Inspector Brissac smiling at me in his calm and knowing way.

"Hello, Mister Slade," Brissac said. "It is such a pleasure to see you again. I hope that we can put an end to this charade. Now that you've turned up."

Brissac turned to Morgan. He asked about Graham and the other British agent, the one called Smith. Morgan said that they'd been taken care of. But there was a certain amount of cleaning up to be done. "The woman drove into town to call Graham's man in Marseille."

Brissac stroked his drooping moustache, in thought. His bare scalp was damp from the rain. Finally he said, "She won't reach him."

Morgan nodded. "Then we're almost done here."

"I think so too," Brissac said.

Morgan smiled. Nodded at me. He seemed to want to reassure me. He seemed to want to convey to me that everything was going to be fine. I would be out of the country soon. I would be safe. But I'll never know for sure what Morgan meant. Because right then Brissac pulled a small revolver out of his overcoat pocket. He raised the revolver and without a word he shot Morgan in the side of the head.

26

I saw the revolver. I heard the shot. I recall vividly the stream of blood. Morgan's legs buckled and he collapsed onto the floor in a heap. As though his bones had disintegrated and his body was now a sack of disconnected tissue.

I stared dumbstruck at Morgan's body. Then I stared dumbstruck at Brissac. Brissac studied the corpse. He nudged it with the toe of his shoe. As though appraising his work with the revolver. As though wondering if it had been an exquisite piece of gunplay or merely a serviceable one. The pool of blood spread out on the carpet under Morgan's body from the wound above his left ear. I saw a neck muscle twitching with the memory of life. Morgan was dead. He wasn't getting up again. I felt my hands shaking. I was sure that Brissac intended to shoot me now too. And there wasn't a thing I could do about it.

"Don't be concerned with him, Mister Slade," Brissac said. "I understand that he was an acquaintance of yours, but he wasn't worth going to a great deal of trouble for. It's best to get him out of the way now. He served his purpose. Just as you have served your purpose. It must be a type of miracle that you are still alive. You've exceeded all expectations."

I saw Brissac's mouth move. I heard the words. They didn't make a great deal of sense to me.

The man standing at the edge of the foyer coughed. I had almost forgotten about him. I noticed that he held a pistol in his hand now too. A large pistol with a black finish and a square outline. His face remained hidden in the shadows. Brissac took a step back and glanced at the other man. Then he tucked the revolver away in his overcoat pocket. He reached into his coat and removed a small black cell phone from an inside pocket. He opened the cover and tapped a button and raised the phone to his ear. Awkwardly, as though he wasn't quite comfortable with the device.

After a moment Brissac frowned.

He turned to the man in the foyer.

"The blocking unit is still on," Brissac said, in French. Impatient. He snapped the phone closed. "Do you know where Morgan positioned it?"

"He was going to place it in the garage," the other man said. His voice sounded like two rocks grinding together. He spoke French with an accent that I didn't recognize. An accent that clipped the ends off his words as though he was biting them off with his teeth. "Are you sure it's still operating?"

"See for yourself then."

Brissac tossed the cell phone to the other man. The man stepped forward out of the shadows. Caught the phone in his free hand. For the first time I saw his face. I saw the deep-set eyes and the flattened nose and the tight skin stretched over his skull-like scar tissue.

It was Verga. The man who Graham had called a monster. A devil.

Arnik Konstantin Verga...

Verga glanced at me without interest. As though he didn't know who I was. He flipped the cover of the phone up. Entered a phone number with his thumb and raised the phone to his ear. The pistol in his other hand remained steady. His eyes were dark and cold. Just two black pinpoints. Floating in the pus-colored whites of his eyes. There was a bandage taped to the side of his neck, and another one, stretched across his forehead, just under the hairline. Must've been from the wounds he received during the ambush in Nice.

Verga cut off the call and redialed. Still nothing. He gave up and closed the phone and tossed it back to Brissac.

"Go to the garage and see if you can find it," Brissac said. "I need to contact the others."

Verga gave Brissac a disgruntled look. His mouth opened but no sound came out. He turned and disappeared into the shadows of the foyer. I heard the front door open and the sounds of the storm grow louder. Then the muffled sound of Verga pulling the door closed behind him as he stepped outside. I can't say that I was unhappy to see him go.

I looked at Brissac. He had the revolver out again. The barrel was pointed at my chest.

"You're not with the police," I said. It came out as a flat statement. I didn't recognize the sound of my own voice.

"In point of fact, I do represent the *Police Nationale*," Brissac said. "I have been in their employ for over twenty years. This comes as a surprise to you?"

I nodded at Morgan's body. The words when I spoke came out of nowhere. "I'm guessing your boss isn't going to be happy about this."

Brissac went on like he hadn't heard me. "Do you know

210

what I learned in those twenty years, Mister Slade? I learned that the people on the so-called right side of the law are no different than the ones on the so-called wrong side. The only difference between the two is that one has the power and authority to get away with their crimes, and the others often do not. Not having been born into privilege or money, it occurred to me some time ago that if I charted a course that allowed me to work on both sides of the law, I could have the best of both worlds. I could act entirely in my own interests, outside of the usual boundaries, and also wield enough power to keep the finger of suspicion from pointing in my direction. It has worked remarkably well."

Brissac smiled. He was pleased with himself. But the smile looked strained. I tried to piece together the bits and bobs of what I knew. All the things that had happened since I arrived in Nice. The details that Graham had given me and the details that Morgan had given me. I fit them into new patterns. The vaguest hint of an idea emerged.

I said, "How long have you worked for the Rising Sun?"

Brissac pursed his lips. Glanced at the ceiling as though he had to think about the question. He said, "It has been over a year now. How quickly time flies." A ponderous tone crept into his voice. "When I was first promoted to this position I had a number of run-ins with the Rising Sun. My superiors—such as they are—wanted my men to track them down and crush them and throw their bones into the sea. When CIA became involved as well, the Rising Sun realized that things were going to be tough for them. And so they approached me with an olive branch. They made the situation clear. Either we were going to be at war with each other—in which case my own life was in grave danger—or we would work together for the mutual good. When I was faced with a choice between certain death or enriching myself in the wildest terms possible, the answer was obvious to me. Life is short, Mister Slade. Why spend it fighting? I have no doubt that you understand that."

"I understand part of it," I said. "You've been using your position to mislead your employers and protect the Rising Sun. But the ambush in Nice—the press reported that it was a Rising Sun operation. Which apparently it was. You wanted to kill me to keep me from talking, and you brought in Verga and his men to do it. That was kind of clumsy, don't you think? Instead of throwing suspicion away from yourself and the Rising Sun, you pulled it right down on top of you."

Brissac shook his head. There was sadness in his expression now. As though I had let him down.

"You've given this some thought," he said. "But not nearly enough. It was actually a perfect move. The truck that was used in our attempt to neutralize you has been traced back to a trucking firm owned by Ali El-Kef. The municipal police in Nice have also found certain pieces of evidence at a rented house that indicate that El-Kef and his men were most certainly behind the attack—I, myself, made sure that it was there for them to find. This information will be released to the press very soon and poor El-Kef will be in no position to deny it. His boat sank in the Mediterranean Sea as he tried to make his way to Algeria. All hands were lost. An unfortunate seafaring accident, but these things happen."

"You can't control everything, Brissac."

"Listen to me, Mister Slade. As we speak, the British are calling even more loudly for the French government to take strong action against the Rising Sun. But when evidence is discovered that proves beyond a doubt that the *contretemps* in Nice was the work of the known thief and smuggler El-Kef—a man who was a tool of MI6, as we are prepared to prove—the British will look even more foolish than they already do. Their ability to influence French domestic security will be effectively over, and the Rising Sun will be free to continue to operate in France. For as long as it pleases me."

The smoke from the fireplace had grown thick again. Brissac didn't seem to notice. He continued to tell me about his secret life and his plans. "The one mistake was that we weren't able to liquidate you in Nice," he said. "You ran faster and farther than I would have ever guessed. You got away from us in Sète, and then also in Marseille, with the help of the British. You are a resourceful man. But I believe that running you to ground right here will work just as well."

Brissac seemed to be enjoying himself. I supposed that he didn't often get a chance to talk about his association with the Rising Sun openly. But he could tell me all about it, because he was sure I'd be dead soon.

But there was a glaring hole in Brissac's plan. I couldn't believe that he didn't see it. "What about Verga?" I said. "Everyone knows that he's tied in with the Rising Sun. The British know and the Americans know. Your own people must know as well. How do you explain that to your superiors?"

"That's the amusing part. On paper, Monsieur Verga is a high level informant that I have cultivated inside the Rising Sun. A double agent, if you will. The truth, of course, is exactly the opposite. I am effectively a double agent for the Rising Sun."

I looked down at the body on the floor. "Did Morgan work for the Rising Sun too?"

"I don't know what Morgan believed himself to be doing. Whatever it was, he did not do it very well."

Brissac glanced up. Smoke from the fireplace drifted across the ceiling. Keeping me in sight Brissac stepped across the room to the front windows. I watched him and wondered if this was my chance. The sofa was only a few feet behind me. The riot gun still lay on the cushions. How long would it take me to turn and dive for the gun and raise it and aim and fire? Too damned long, I was sure.

But if I was ever going to try it, I needed to do it soon. Before Verga returned.

Brissac reached the windows. Keeping me covered with the revolver he pulled the curtain aside with his free hand and glanced out the window. I didn't imagine that he could see much. Rain washed down the window glass. The sky was still dark. I wondered what time it was. I wondered if Aurora was coming back. I hoped that she wasn't. I hoped that she'd driven right through Valence and kept on driving. Heading north to Paris and then farther still, until she reached Calais or Boulogne and crossed the channel. I hoped that she was running as fast as she'd ever run in her life. But it was only wishful thinking. Aurora had no idea what had happened here. The trap had been sprung and now she was going to walk right into it. And that would be the end of both of us.

Brissac let go of the curtain. It fell back into place.

"Mister Slade," he said. Motioning for me to approach the window. "Please."

The barrel of the revolver followed me as I crossed the room. I stepped over to the window. I could hear a vehicle approaching in low gear. The sound grew louder.

"Take a look," Brissac said. "Tell me if that is your

214

companion."

I took hold of the curtain in my left hand and pulled it aside and peered out of the window. I saw a dim pair of headlights slicing through the rain. Through the wet glass the lights looked diffuse and unsteady, like two lanterns swinging in the night.

I said, "I don't know if that's her or not. I can't see it clearly."

I heard Brissac moving behind me. A second later I was hit on the back of the head. The force of the blow pushed me forward and my forehead hit the vertical edge of the window sill hard and my left hand, still gripping the curtain, wound up pressed against my chest. I righted myself. I felt the muzzle of the pistol being pressed into the back of my neck. My first thought was that he'd hit me with the butt of the revolver. But no, it hadn't been that kind of blow. He'd punched me in the back of the head with his fist. Maybe he thought my attention was drifting. Maybe he just wanted to hit something.

"Look more closely, Mister Slade."

It was right then that I changed my tack. I decided to play along. Tell Brissac what he wanted to know. I continued to hold the curtain close to my chest as I gave Brissac every detail. The truck left the dirt road, and I told him that. Now it was pulling onto the gravel in front of the villa, and I told him that too. The truck stopped and the engine died out and the driver's door opened. I gave Brissac a running description. He must've thought the blow to my head had dislodged something important, up there in my cranium.

Aurora climbed out of the truck. I caught a glimpse of her outline in the darkness as she ran through the rain to the front door. She should've been running in the other direction. She shouldn't have returned at all.

"She's coming to the door now," I said.

Brissac grabbed the back of my collar. He pulled me away from the window. I'd been expecting that, or something like that. Brissac seemed to want me to move in the direction of the foyer and the front door.

But I had other plans.

Standing at the window, holding the curtain close to my chest, I had slid the paring knife out of the chest pocket of my boiler suit. The knife that Graham had handed to me to cut the washing line cord we had used to tie up Nightingale's body. I'd slid the knife into my chest pocket when I was done cutting the cord, then forgotten about it. Until I felt it there after Brissac hit me and I fell forward.

Now it was in my left hand. With my fingers around the handle and the four-inch blade pointed down, toward the floor. As Brissac again pulled hard on my collar to pull me away from the window I pretended to stumble backwards. Brissac tried to step aside to keep me from falling into him but he was too slow and I was too close. His gun hand waved in the air as he tried to get it behind me but I was too close for that too. I pivoted hard on my heel and thrust the knife backwards. With every bit of strength that I had.

I hit him low in the stomach.

The knife sliced through cloth. It cut into flesh.

I twisted the blade.

Brissac made a noise like a soft grunt. I hadn't expected to hurt him greatly. Just surprise him. And buy myself a few seconds of time. As he fell backwards with the force of the knife blow he tried to bring the pistol around but I was still too close to him. I let go of the knife handle and spun to the left, toward the pistol hand. I grabbed Brissac's wrist with both of my hands and pushed the arm up until the pistol barrel was pointed at the ceiling. Then I ducked under the arm and twisted it around and down and kept twisting.

I felt something give.

Brissac screamed.

The pistol fell to the floor.

I'd broken his arm.

I let go of the arm and Brissac stumbled backwards a few feet. I looked around for the pistol on the floor. It had slid behind the bottom edge of the window curtain. I fumbled with the curtain and pulled it aside and reached down and picked up the pistol. As I straightened up I saw Brissac coming toward me. He had pulled the paring knife out of his stomach with his good hand and now he lashed out with the blade, swinging it in a wide arc toward my head as he dove toward me.

I raised the pistol. There wasn't time to aim.

The sound of the gunshot pounded my ears. The kick of the pistol jolted me. Time slowed down. Brissac seemed to hang in the air. His eyes wide open. An expression of profound surprise pasted on his face. Momentum kept him lunging forward. I ducked to one side even as I saw the small dark mark on his neck and wondered if it was enough to stop him. He hit the wall to one side of the window and then slid down the wall and came to rest on the floor.

For a moment his good arm was stretched out above his head, as though he was looking for a handhold to keep him from falling farther. Then the arm slid slowly down the wall. A deep liquid sound came from his throat. Blood filled his mouth and flowed down his chin.

From the way he landed I could see the dark ragged hole at the back of his neck.

The glazed eyes didn't move.

Brissac was dead.

I looked up. Aurora stood at the edge of the foyer. Her eyes moved from me to the dead man on the floor beside me, and then to the other corpse, near the couch. She clasped her hand over her mouth. Her eyes were open wide with fear.

I moved quickly toward her.

"Verga is here," I said. "He'll kill us. We've got to get out."

Aurora pulled her arm out of my grip. She cried out. I grabbed her roughly and turned her around. I pushed her back into the foyer and toward the open doorway.

We stumbled out into the storm. The cool rain felt good on my face. I pulled Aurora along with me and we ran toward the truck. I can't say why, with all that was going on, but I suddenly realized that the bulk under her boiler suit was gone.

She wasn't wearing the bulletproof vest.

I pulled up and grabbed her by the shoulders.

"Where's the vest?" I had to shout over the noise of the storm. Aurora didn't seem to hear. Her eyes seemed focused on a point far off. I shook her hard. Trying to bring her back to the here and now.

She said, "I left it in the truck." She wiped wet hair away from her eyes as the rain pelted us and the wind threatened to knock us down. "Where is Graham? Tell me."

"She's dead. They shot her."

Aurora shook her head. She didn't want to believe it. I grabbed her arm and we proceeded on toward the truck. Our heads down in the rain. We'd worry about the crumbling state of our mental faculties some other time. Right now we had to make a run for it.

As we reached the truck my foot slipped in the wet gravel. Instinctively I reached toward the truck for a handhold to keep myself from falling but my hand slid off the surface of the hood and I fell backward and landed on the ground. I rolled onto my side and as I got to my feet I glanced toward the front of the house.

At that same moment Verga appeared. He paused in the front doorway. His face was half in the shadows and half in the dull light of the foyer. He peered out into the storm. He gripped his pistol and when he saw us beside the truck he swung the pistol toward us. His face looked pale and waxy. Like the pallor of a man who was already dead.

27

Verga must've attended to his business out at the garage and reentered the house through the kitchen door. He'd crossed the main hall. He'd seen his boss dead on the floor.

Now he was looking for something to shoot.

I turned and ran around the side of the truck. Aurora stood next to the open driver's door. I heard a dull popping sound on the wind. Then a sharp clattering as a bullet hit the truck's front grill and disappeared into the engine compartment.

Aurora looked at me blankly. She didn't seem to realize that we had just been shot at. A second round hit the front of the truck just as I raised Brissac's pistol.

I pointed the pistol in the direction of the front door and fired.

It was a wild shot. Probably didn't come close to Verga. But I wanted him to know that I was armed too. It might slow him down. And slowing him down for a second or two was about the best we could hope for under the circumstances.

I realized that we couldn't use the truck. We'd be shot before we had the engine started. We had to run. I grabbed Aurora and pushed her forward once more. For a moment we were hidden from Verga's view by the truck's cargo box. I looked ahead at the sheets of rain streaming down. There was no place to run to. But we couldn't stay here. Any second now Verga was going to jump off the porch. Run out into the gravel. He'd come around the front of the truck and start firing.

We ran around the back of the truck. Ahead of us was the side of the villa where Nightingale's BMW stood. Forty feet to the right of the BMW was the old well. Beyond them both was the low stone wall at the edge of the vineyard. The ground at the side of the villa was mud. I pulled Aurora along and we ran hell-bent across the fifteen feet of open space between the truck and the corner of the villa. I kept the pistol pointed toward the villa's front steps.

When we were halfway across the open space I fired off another round. I caught a glimpse of Verga crouched down in the doorway with his own pistol raised.

I saw the pistol buck in his hand.

His shot missed its mark and we reached the cover of the villa. My mind raced. We didn't have many options. Perhaps we could run around the villa to the garage. Lock ourselves inside. Hole up there. At least until the ammunition ran out. That would buy us time. Maybe we could wait Verga out. Or would he call in reinforcements? I thought of Graham. Her body was out there somewhere. Perhaps we could find her phone and use it to call the local police. Now that the blocking device was turned off. She'd also had a pistol with her when she stepped out into the storm—was it still tucked away in her boiler suit? It was a slim hope but I clung to it.

We moved as fast as we dared to in the mud. It was only then that I remembered the shotgun lying on the sofa. I'd forgotten about it entirely in my haste to get out of the house.

It was one of many mistakes.

We were alongside Nightingale's car now. Our feet slipped and slid as I pulled Aurora along with me. She gasped for breath. I looked past her shoulder. Expecting to see Verga behind us. Then I realized that Aurora was carrying something. I hadn't noticed before. For a split second I thought it was a jacket, but it wasn't.

It was the bulletproof vest.

She must've pulled it out of the truck. I'd asked about it and so she'd retrieved it and brought it along. Thinking that I wanted it. Thinking that it might be useful. The vest hung limp in her hand. The bottom edge dragged in the mud. If what Morgan had said was true, then one unlucky shot from Verga and Aurora and I would be blown skyward. Bits and pieces of us would fall back to earth with the rain.

I reached out and tore the vest from her hand.

Ahead of us was the low stone wall at the edge of the vineyard. I pushed Aurora toward it. As we struggled forward in the mud I tossed the vest toward the dark mouth of the stone well.

It could join Graham's other vest at the bottom.

We reached the wall just as Verga appeared, crouched down, at the corner of the house. We dove for cover and landed in the mud on the other side of the wall with our backs up against the wooden trellises that held the grape vines. Aurora started to raise herself up on her hands and knees but I pulled her back down.

The stone wall was three feet high. High enough to give us cover, as long as we stayed reasonably close to the ground. We lay there. We caught our breath. I counted our blessings and didn't get further than one—we were still alive. The darkness and the slanting rain seemed to push us down farther into the mud.

It was only a matter of time before Verga crept up on us. How many rounds did I have left? I found a button toward the top of the pistol butt and pushed it. The magazine popped down from the bottom edge of the butt. I pulled it out completely and studied it. A narrow slot that ran the height of the magazine allowed me to count the cartridges. I saw three, slotted in one on top of the other, at the top end of the magazine. And there was a fourth cartridge in the chamber of the pistol.

Four shots. Four chances to stop Verga before he stopped us.

The odds on our side looked long but there was nothing to be done about it. I looked at Aurora. I knew that she understood too, that we'd reached the end of our luck. She tried to smile. I saw tears in the corners of her eyes. They mixed with the rain drops.

I pulled her close and whispered in her ear.

"Crawl along the wall," I said. "Get to the garage. Graham is dead. Her body is out there by the garage somewhere. Find her and get her cell phone and her pistol. Then get inside the garage and lock it up and call the police. Tell them there is a madman out here with a gun. Three people are dead. That should catch their interest. Don't leave the garage until the police arrive."

Aurora shook her head. She didn't like it but I convinced her. I told her that we hadn't come this far just to give up. The weak smile fell from her face. She raised her chin and leaned in and kissed me on the forehead. It was a muddy kiss, but it was a kiss.

I told her to get moving.

Aurora started off. Crawling forward in the mud. All elbows and knees. After a few seconds of clumsiness she got the hang of it and proceeded forward about as fast as anyone could. I watched her for a moment to make sure that she kept herself under the top of the wall and out of Verga's line of fire.

I'm not heroic. I stayed behind to keep Verga busy because it was the only thing I could do. We were in the last ditch. If Aurora didn't make it across the vineyard to the garage then we would both be dead soon.

But she'd make it, I told myself.

I raised myself up and peered over the top of the wall. Verga was nowhere in sight. Then I caught a glimpse of his dark figure through the windows of Nightingale's BMW. Verga had ducked behind the back of the car. He'd been waiting. I raised the pistol to fire but he spotted me and ducked down farther and disappeared before I could get a shot off. I ducked back down too. When I peered over the wall once more I thought Verga was still behind the rear of the car. I was caught off-guard when his head popped up beside the driver's door, between the car and the side of the house.

He fired.

The round ricocheted off the top of the stone wall. Chips of rock hit me in the face as I ducked. It was close. An inch or two to the right and I'd have been finished. The round would have ricocheted right into my forehead. Without raising my head to look I reached up and fired a round blindly. Just to push Verga back behind the car. I didn't want him to get comfortable. Then I crawled along the wall to the right for several feet at double speed. He'd be expecting me to reappear in the same spot. Changing my position behind the wall might throw him off for a moment.

I had three cartridges left.

I waited a few seconds. Then I raised myself up. I didn't see any movement out there. I rested the butt of the pistol on the wall and kept it aimed at the car. The dark sky was like a heavy blanket over the landscape. The relentless rain lashed at my face.

Then Verga showed his face. But not where I thought he would. He'd returned to the rear of the car. He peered out from behind the BMW and dropped to one knee and took aim. I ducked below the wall just as he fired. I huddled there, relieved to find that my head was still attached to my shoulders.

I looked down the line of the wall.

Through the blinding rain I could just make out Aurora in the distance. She was on her feet now. She was running in a crouch along the stone wall, her movements unsteady in the mud. She only had a short way to go before she reached the end of the wall and could make a break across the open ground to the garage.

But I still needed to keep Verga busy.

I crawled back to the left and stopped six feet beyond my original position. I took a deep breath and raised my head and peered over the wall.

Verga was just stepping out from behind the car. In a crouch, with his pistol raised. He looked like he intended to run toward the well, which was roughly forty feet from the car and twenty feet in front of me. Making for the well was the logical move. But he needed time to traverse the large patch of mud between Nightingale's car and the well and I'd caught him before he could start.

For a fraction of a second I saw the deep-set eyes burning inside the skull-like face. I thought I was staring at death itself.

I fired.

Verga scrambled back behind the car.

A wasted shot. Two cartridges left.

I rested the butt of the pistol on the top of the stone wall and steadied it in both hands. The next shot was going to have to do some damage. I couldn't afford to miss.

Then I saw something I hadn't noticed before. It gave me an idea. Not much of an idea. A definite longshot. But right now everything looked like a longshot. I wondered if it was even longer a shot than I imagined. Because at the center of this idea was the fact that when Verga showed himself I intended to hold my fire. I wanted him to get to the well. Or, at least, close to it.

I held the pistol steady in my hands. I rested my arms on the stone wall. The harsh rattle of the rain grew louder.

I waited.

The flashes of lightning became brighter. The rumble of thunder started deep inside my bones and curved up my spine and shook my skull.

I waited.

My heartbeat pulsed in my ears. It was louder than the pounding rain.

I waited.

I noticed the tips of my fingers had turned a curious shade of blue.

I waited some more.

Time stopped. The world was reduced to my shallow breathing and the vapor that my warm breath left in the cold air and the blinding rain and the cold steel in my hands.

Then it happened.

Verga broke cover. He darted out from behind the car and fired one shot and kept moving. There was forty feet of mud in front of him and he was headed straight for the cover of the well. He fired again, a wild shot intended to make me duck down behind the wall.

But I didn't duck.

I could see that he was struggling to keep his balance in the mud. He was moving fast, but erratically. I didn't have a clean shot at him—he remained partly hidden behind the stone well. But that was all right. I wasn't looking for a clean shot at him. Not anymore. No doubt, Verga made a fine target, to someone who was good with a pistol. But I wasn't that person. So I didn't aim at Verga. I aimed at a point slightly forward and to the left of Verga. Twenty feet in front of me.

I aimed at the stone well. And Aurora's bulletproof vest.

I thought I had tossed it into the well but the vest had caught on one of the iron posts. The posts that had once held the crossbar for a well bucket. Just like my own vest had when I had tried to throw it into the well earlier. Aurora's vest hung from the post like it was hanging from a coat hook. The blustery wind pushed it this way and that. The vest glistened black in the rain.

Morgan had said that the plastic explosives in the vest were generally stable. Only a detonator could be counted on to set them off. And Morgan had showed me where the embedded detonator was. At the front of the vest. High on the left side. He'd also suggested that a gunshot to the detonator might set off an explosion. And right now it was the left side of the vest that lay exposed as it hung from the rough iron post of the well. If I could hit the detonator in the vest and cause it to set off the plastic explosive charges, and if the explosion was strong enough, it might take Verga out of the fight. For good.

The vest wasn't a stationary target because of the wind, but it was more stationary than Verga was. And it was only twenty feet away. And it was right out in the open. I had no idea how good my chances of hitting the vest in just the right place were, but I was sure they were better than my chances of picking off Verga. The odds that I could beat a professional gunman at his own game had never been good, or even mediocre. All of these thoughts raced around in my head as I took careful aim at the spot on the front of the vest where Morgan had said the detonator was.

Then I fired.

The vest canted to the left for a moment. Then it canted back to the right. But that was just the wind pushing it. Nothing else happened. Except that, beyond the well, Verga ducked his head lower and hunched his shoulders even more at the sound of the gunshot. But he continued running.

I fired a second time.

The vest jumped and spun.

I'd hit it. I couldn't tell where, but I'd hit it.

For a second I thought the vest was going to fall off the post entirely and disappear into the well. But it continued to wave back and forth in the air. In smaller and smaller arcs. Then it settled back down.

Nothing else happened.

I had missed the detonator. With both rounds. Either that, or Morgan had been wrong and there were no explosives in the vest. But there was no time to wonder about it. A patch of stone wall kicked up in my face. Verga had slipped and fallen in the mud. From where he now lay he had a clean shot at me. And I now had a clean shot at him. A lucky break after all. Instinctively I aimed the pistol at his prone outline and pulled the trigger.

The hammer fell on an empty chamber.

The magazine was empty.

I can't credit the idea that Verga heard the hollow clicking sound. I don't see how he could have, over the noise of the storm. But somehow he sensed that I was done. And he was right. I thought I saw a deathly smile spread across Verga's face as he climbed to his feet in the mud.

He'd won.

I scrambled to my right. In the direction that Aurora had gone. There was nothing left to do but run.

But I didn't get far.

Suddenly the ground shook under my feet. I was thrown off balance and I fell against the wall. I landed along the top of it with my arms stretched out. I caught a glimpse of the stone well as I struggled to get behind the wall. I saw the great spout of smoke and sound and debris that erupted from the well and pushed upward and to either side and roiled in the air. It grew still larger and still taller. Then the percussive force of the explosion knocked me back behind the wall and onto the ground. The sound of the explosion reverberated across the hillside behind me and then rolled back down, like a booming wave of noise that crashed up on a rocky shore, then receded back into the ocean.

I closed my eyes tight and wrapped my arms over my head to protect myself from falling pieces of stone and earth.

One of my shots had hit the mark after all. There had been some sort of delayed detonation. I didn't know the science of it and I didn't care. It had happened, and I was grateful.

After a moment the landscape stopped falling on me. I risked looking up over the wall. The stone well had disintegrated. It simply wasn't there any longer. I saw heavy drifting smoke that was already dissipating in the rain. The side of the BMW that had faced the well was blackened and the windows were shattered. The smoke rolled over the car and climbed the side of the villa.

No one near the well could have survived the blast.

Verga was dead.

I coughed and squinted my eyes in the smoke. I felt relief wash over me.

Then Verga stepped out of an eddy of smoke.

He walked quite deliberately. He held his right arm straight out in front of him. The pistol gripped in his right hand was steady. He appeared in the curling smoke right about where the structure of the well had been. His face was blackened and cut and bleeding. His clothes were torn.

I froze. I thought I was seeing a ghost.

Verga stopped when he saw me. He set both feet firmly in the mud and swung the pistol toward me. It was a machine-like movement. He looked dazed. I saw blood trailing out of his ears. His eyes were also the color of blood but somehow brighter. I thought I could see the fires of hell reflected in them.

The pistol barrel rose an inch or two.

His finger tightened on the trigger.

Then the earth exploded again. A great column of roiling smoke shot from the hole in the ground where the well had been. The cloud grew wider as it shot upward. Like a bolt of bright white flame.

I was thrown to the muddy ground again. I covered my head again. I waited for the landscape to stop falling on me again. I noticed that there was less falling landscape this time.

It must've been the other vest exploding. The first one. The vest that I'd thrown into the well earlier, at Morgan's direction.

I picked myself up off the ground again. I looked around and took stock. A large blackened pile of bloodied flesh and cloth lay several yards from the hole in the ground. Not far from the wreckage of the car.

It was Verga. What was left of him.

The first explosion had caused the other vest to explode as well. Some kind of sympathetic explosion—I believe that is the correct terminology. In any case, it was sympathetic to me. It had saved my ass. I studied the remains on the ground. I gave Verga a minute to screw himself together and come at me one more time. But he couldn't do it.

He stayed dead.

I glanced up. There was a dark hole along the edge of the villa's roof. The hole was surrounded by crushed clay tiles and flames licked up from the hole. I watched the flames grow. That the villa could catch fire in the middle of a biblical rainstorm wasn't an acutely funny notion but I laughed and kept laughing until my chest hurt and I couldn't laugh anymore and I wanted to cry. I pulled myself together as best I could. Let the villa burn. Let it and the vineyards and Valence and Lyon and all of France and the whole of the so-called civilized world burn to the ground.

I had to find Aurora.

28

Aurora and I needed a fast car. We appropriated the Mercedes-Benz that Brissac and Verga had arrived in and drove west, toward Aurillac and Cahors.

We ditched the boiler suits at a truck stop near the A75 highway and reached Toulouse at nightfall. We left the Mercedes parked on a dark side street and two hours later we sat on a train heading south, toward the Spanish frontier. Aurora was certain that her uncle in Cerbère could put us up for a few days.

We could rest there and take stock of our situation.

The train pulled into Cerbère just before dawn. The uncle's house was a twenty-minute walk from the station, on a hillside overlooking the sea. His name was Emil. He smiled warmly at Aurora and gave me a suspicious once-over. His wife was a stout woman named Fiona. She fussed at the kitchen stove and made Aurora and I coffee and *oeufs aux herbes* with fried bread while we sat at the kitchen table talking to her husband.

Aurora made it clear to Emil that she and I might be in a little trouble with the French authorities. A misunderstanding, of course, but we needed to get out of the country until we could get it cleared up. Emil wasn't bothered so much by the tale. He seemed like a man who'd fallen afoul of the law once or twice himself. But when Aurora floated the idea of Emil taking us to Tangier on his fishing boat, Emil frowned and held his hands out, palms up—the universal gesture for nothing doing. Emil's two sons—Aurora's cousins—had taken the boat south to the island of Mallorca, off the east coast of Spain. They were bricklayers by trade and had contracted to do some work for a Spanish construction firm there. They'd be gone for at least two more days.

The aunt gave Emil a worried look and folded her arms. Emil asked why we couldn't drive across the frontier into Spain and continue on south, to Malaga or Marbella. From there we could hire a boat for the trip to Tangier. It was a reasonable suggestion and one that Aurora and I had considered earlier. The Spanish frontier was only a stone's throw away, and it was normally wide open these days. But there was the risk that the French police were watching the roads. And even if we managed to cross the frontier, there was no guarantee that the Spanish police weren't keeping an eye out for us inside Spain.

Aurora and I decided to pin our hopes on the fishing boat for the time being. Emil nodded and sighed. If that was our decision, he said, then the least he could do was to let us hole up in the guest cottage behind the house while we waited for the cousins to return.

The aunt frowned. She said nothing.

The guest cottage stood two hundred feet up the hillside, at the edge of a copse of trees. We could see clearly the rolling brown hills of the coastline to the north and south and the long rocky beach to the east and the white-capped waves of the sea. The aunt walked behind us carrying fresh sheets for the beds, a towel and washcloth, and a wicker basket with bread and cheese and a bottle of red wine.

Aurora and I slept until late afternoon. We awoke to find Emil sitting at the table next to the cottage's front window. He was drinking a bottle of Spanish beer and reading that day's edition of *La Vanguardia*. Emil shook his head when he saw me. His smile was deep and seemed to be carved out of the same dark rock that dotted the hillside around us. He told us he'd driven down to the border crossing while we'd slept. Just to have a look around.

"Your instincts were correct," he said. "The French police have set up a checkpoint. The cars are backed up for several miles. I wouldn't advise trying to drive into Spain."

Aurora stood at the window. "Could they know that we're in the area?"

Emil shrugged and said anything was possible. Aurora fell silent and shook her head.

Nothing was decided.

"I'll leave the newspaper for you," Emil said. "You can read about yourself." Then Emil pulled an old revolver out of a canvas sack he'd brought with him. It was accompanied by a box of .32 caliber cartridges. "I'll leave this also. There are wild dogs that roam the hills. At night they come right up to the cottage looking for food. They are mean and not afraid of anything."

I hefted the pistol in my hand. It was lightweight. The box of cartridges was full.

"The only thing for wild dogs is to shoot them," Emil said as he left.

Aurora read the newspaper report to me in English. The facts, such as they were, were wrapped up in lurid prose. According to the newspaper I had murdered Brissac and Morgan at the "house of blood" outside of Valence, then tried to burn the house down to hide the details of my heinous crime. Apparently I was now not only a murderer but a firebug. Police organizations throughout France and Spain were on high alert. Responsible citizens were advised to report any sighting of me to the nearest constabulary. Aurora was mentioned in the report but not by name, and her part in my alleged crimes was not made clear. There was no mention at all of Morgan or Graham, Nightingale or Verga.

The omissions make me wonder. Perhaps the police don't know what to make of those details and have decided to leave them out for now. Or perhaps they do know what to make of them and plan to leave them out for good. And it wouldn't be unworkable. All they have to do is keep us quiet. That's not a Herculean task, considering all the people who are looking for us. The French Central Directorate and the *Police Nationale*. The CIA and the British Secret Intelligence Service. The mobsters and terrorists of the Rising Sun. And El-Kef's men, the ones who were left behind in Sète. All of them, no doubt, would like a quiet word with us. I'm under no misconception that any of these people will let us live.

We know too much, that's the long and the short of it.

They want us dead.

What chance do we have of surviving? I don't kid myself that our prospects are good. They're not even fair to middling. So I decided to write all of this down. If we should happen to disappear off the face of the earth soon I want to leave a record of this behind. I want people to know how things were and how they unraveled. I want people to know what the guardians of all that is good and true are doing when they're not sleeping the sleep of the just. I started writing this in pencil, but Emil brought me this portable typewriter from the house. Along with a ream of paper and an ink ribbon that isn't fresh. A month ago I would've written poems on this typewriter. But that state of mind seems to belong to a time long ago. Morgan told me that the world doesn't need any more poems. What it needs is more guns. Maybe he was right. I hope that he wasn't but I fear that he was.

It's been four days now and still the cousins have not returned from Mallorca. Emil can't even reach them on the phone. I have to wonder if they've encountered trouble of some kind. I keep watching the coastline, trying to make the boat appear through the sheer force of my will.

Maybe the boat will arrive too late.

Maybe it will never come.

Emil came to the cottage this evening and told us that he'd seen men in town that afternoon. Men he'd never seen before. There were three of them and they wore suits and drove into the town square in a dark sedan. They fanned out and talked to whoever they could find. After a while they left again—Emil assured us that he saw them depart with his own eyes. But there was a rueful expression on his face as he told us all of this. It was clear to me that he was having second thoughts about hiding us in the cottage.

Aurora is asleep in the bedroom now. She didn't say much today. The strain of staying out of sight in this cottage is starting to show. Even the whistling of the wind as it blows in off the sea is working on my nerves. Earlier tonight, around dusk, I heard noises outside. Soft voices. The sound of a car engine in the distance. They seemed to come from behind the cottage. Somewhere in the darkness of the trees. I jumped up and grabbed the revolver. The lights were off in the kitchen and I pushed the edge of the window curtain to one side with my finger and peered out. I half expected to see a squad of policemen surrounding the cottage, with a trio of men in smart suits giving the orders. But I didn't see anything. And the noises had ceased. I opened the window a crack and listened. Still nothing. Just the fading light and the sea breeze and the dark clouds over the trees. My ears were playing tricks.

I've already decided that if the boat doesn't arrive tomorrow we'll have to find another route south. Maybe into the mountains to the west and then down into central Spain. Move slowly across the countryside and try to blend in. We can make it work if we have to, and we have to. Right now the thought of reaching Tangier is everything. We'll have room to breathe there. Room to think clearly. We will rest there. We will find a few days of peace. And once we have rested I will go to the American embassy in Rabat and tell them everything. We have to hide in plain sight. Graham was right about that much. I don't want to disappear into a dungeon jail cell in Tangier and there it is I just heard it again—

The bastards, here they come.

CPSIA information can be obtained
at www.ICGtesting.com
Printed in the USA
LVOW08s2022211116
513936LV00003B/239/P